CW00822620

The Hawthorns / a Story About Children

Amy Walton

Chapter One.

Easney Vicarage.

Quite close to the nursery window at Easney Vicarage there grew a very old pear-tree. It was so old that the ivy had had time to hug its trunk with strong rough arms, and even to stretch them out nearly to the top, and hang dark green wreaths on every bough. Some day, the children had been told, this would choke the life out of the tree and kill it; that would be a pity, but there seemed no danger of it yet, for every spring the pear-tree still showed its head crowned with white blossoms, and every summer the pears grew yellow and juicy, and fell with a soft "splosh!" on the gravel path beneath. It was interesting to watch that, and it happened so often, that it was hard to imagine a windsor pear without a great gash where the sharp stones had cut into it; it was also natural to expect when you picked it up that there would be a cunning yellow wasp hidden somewhere about it, for all the little Hawthorns had always found it so except the baby, and she was too small to have any experience. Five little Hawthorns, without counting the baby, had looked out of the nursery window and watched the pear-tree blossom, and the sparrows build their nests, and the pears fall; but by the time this story begins, four of them, whose names were Penelope, Ambrose, Nancy, and David, were schoolroom children, and learnt lessons of Miss Grey down-stairs. They had no longer much time for looking out of the window, and the nursery was left in the possession of Dickie and Cicely the baby. Dickie, whose real name was Delicia, was three years old—a great girl now she thought—but she was still fond of kneeling up in the window seat and flattening her little nose against the glass. She could not see very much. Through the branches of the pear-tree a little to the left appeared the church tower, and a glimpse here and there of grey and white tombstones in the churchyard. Straight in front of her there was a broad lawn sloping down to a sunk fence, and beyond that a meadow with tall elms in it, and after that another meadow where cows were feeding, and that was all. In the spring the meadows turned to gold and silver with the buttercups and daisies, and the rooks cawed noisily in the elms; but in the summer it was all very green and very quiet. Particularly at lesson time, when the "others" were busy with Miss Grey, and Dickie must not make a noise because baby was asleep. Then there was only Andrew to be seen in the distance, bending over his barrow or rake or spade; but he never looked up to the nursery window, and this was not surprising, for Andrew had a great deal to do. He worked in the garden, and fed the chickens, and took care of Ruby the horse, and sometimes drove the wagonette into Nearminster; he also rang the church bell, and was parish clerk. Perhaps it was because he had so much on his mind that he was of a melancholy disposition, and seldom disposed for conversation with the children.

They thought it a pity sometimes that neither the nursery nor the schoolroom window looked out to the front of the house, for it was only a little way back from the street; not that there was much going on in the village, but still you could hear the "clink, clink" from the blacksmith's forge opposite, and see anyone passing the white gate which led out into the road. The vicarage was an old house; many and many a vicar had lived in it, and altered or added to it according to his liking, so that it was full of twists and turns, inside and out, and had wonderful nooks and corners, and strange cupboards under the stairs. Pennie, who was eleven years old, and a great hand at "making up," thought a good deal about those old bygone vicars, and founded some of her choicest romances upon them. There was one particular vicar, a tablet to whose memory was placed in the chancel just opposite the Hawthorns' seat in church.

"Godfrey Ablewhite, sometime vicar of this parish," etcetera.

It seemed to Pennie, as she sat staring up at this during her father's sermons, that she saw plainly what sort of man this Godfrey Ablewhite had been. He was broad and strong, and rode a tall white horse, and had doubtless built those large stables at the vicarage, because he was fond of hunting. From this she would go on to adorn his character with many daring feats of horsemanship, and by the time the sermon was over there was another story ready to be eagerly listened to by the other children—and, indeed, believed also, for they had an infinite trust in Pennie. This was partly because she was the eldest, and partly because she "made up" so well, and had such good ideas about games and plans. No one could make a better plan than Pennie if she put her mind to it, and this was a valuable faculty, for toys were not plentiful at Easney Vicarage, and the children had to find their own amusements. These, fortunately, did not depend upon anything to be bought in shops, for there was only one in the village, and that was the post-office too. There you could get bacon, and peppermint drops, and coarse grey stockings; but for anything more interesting you had to drive to Nearminster, ten miles away. Mother went over there sometimes, and took each child with her in turn, but even then there was a serious drawback to buying much, and that was want of money.

Some children would doubtless think living at Easney a very dull affair. No shops, nothing new to play with, and very little new to wear. Pennie *did* get a little tired sometimes of always wearing serge in winter and holland in summer; but neither she nor her brothers and sisters ever found their lives dull. They would have been astonished at the idea. There were so many interesting things to do. For instance, there was a large family of pet beasts and birds, some living in the barn in cages, and some free. Snuff the terrier was the most intimate and friendly of these last, and Methuselah the tortoise the greatest stranger. The children regarded him with respectful awe, for he passed so much of his life hidden away in the cold dark earth, that he must know many strange and wonderful things which went on there; but, like all people of really wide experience, he was singularly modest and retiring in his behaviour, and appeared on the border the first mild day in spring after his disappearance, with no fuss at all, and as if he had done nothing remarkable.

Pennie's jackdaw, a forward bird, who hopped about with an air of understanding everything, was one day found perched on the tortoise's shell with the evident intention of making some searching inquiries. Methuselah, however, had very prudently drawn in his head, and Jack was both baffled and disgraced.

Next to the animals in point of interest came the Wilderness. This was a part of the garden shut off from the rest by a shrubbery, and given up to the children as their very own. Here they messed and muddled to their hearts' content, carried out a great many interesting designs, and reared quantities of mustard and cress; once they each had a garden, but Nancy, Ambrose, and David had lately struck out the bold idea of joining their plots of ground and digging a well. It was a delightful occupation, and when the hole got deep it was pleasant to see how the small frogs and other slimy reptiles crawled about at the bottom; but, after much heated labour, there were no signs of water. Interest flagged then, and the well was deserted, until the ever-ready Pennie suggested the game of Joseph and his brethren, and it became a favourite amusement to lower Dickie down in a basket amongst the frogs and newts. Dickie was both small and brave, two very necessary qualities for her part, for the basket was narrow, and wobbled about a good deal in its descent; but she was used to perilous positions, and had a soul above fear.

The Wilderness was certainly very interesting; nevertheless at a certain time in the summer it was completely forsaken, and that was when the hay was down. Then everyone must help to get it in; and there could be no lessons done, for even Miss Grey was in the hay-field. Then the excited children, with flushed faces, worked as hard as though the whole matter depended on them alone, and even Dickie, with tiny rake and sturdy legs planted wide apart, did brave service. Then the maids, with sun-bonnets tilted well forward on their foreheads, came out to toss a little hay, and giggle a great deal, and say how hot it was; then the surly Andrew threw sour looks of scorn at them, and the vicar, casting aside his black coat, did more real work than anyone. Then mother came into the field with Cicely in her arms, and was welcomed with acclamations, and forthwith seated on a royal throne of hay; then, under her watchful eyes, the ambitious Ambrose worked feverishly, and threw his arms and legs about like an excited spider. Then Nancy laughed at him, and David pushed him down, and Pennie covered him with hay; and it got into his eyes and down his throat and he choked and kicked, and mother said: "That will do, children!" Then tea was brought out and laid under the great oak-tree, and everyone's face was very red, and everyone was very thirsty. And then the cool evening came stealing on, and a tiny breeze blew, and the hay smelt sweet, and the shadows lengthened, and it was bed-time just as things were getting pleasant.

Each time all this happened it was equally delightful, and

it seemed a pity when the field stood bare and desolate after the hay was carried, shorn of its shadowy grass and pretty flowers; yet there was consolation too in the size of the stack which the children had helped to make, and which they always thought "bigger than last year."

Soon after this autumn came and made the orchard and woods and lanes interesting with apples and nuts and blackberries; and then, after the apples and nuts had been stored away, and the blackberries made into jam, it was time to look forward to the winter.

Winter brought a great deal that was very pleasant; for sometimes he came with snow and ice, and the children would wake up to find that in the night he had quietly covered everything out-of-doors with a sparkling white garment.

Then what could be more delicious than to make a snow man or a snow palace?

Pennie, who was a great reader, and always anxious to carry out something she had read about, inclined towards the palace; but the others had less lofty minds. It quite contented them to make a snow man, to put one of Andrew's pipes in his mouth and a battered hat on his head, and stick in bits of coal for his eyes.

"Isn't he lovely?" Nancy would exclaim when all these adornments were complete.

"Zovely!" echoed Dickie, clapping red worsted mittens ecstatically.

"I think he's rather vulgar," Pennie said doubtfully on one of these occasions with an anxiously puckered brow; "and besides, there's nothing to make up about him. What can you pretend?"

The snow man certainly looked hopelessly prosaic as

Ambrose tilted his hat a little more to one side.

"Guy Fawkes?" suggested David, having studied the matter solidly for some minutes.

"No," said Pennie, "not Guy Fawkes—he's so common—we've had him heaps of times. But I'll tell you what would be splendid; we'll make him a martyr in Smithfield."

The boys looked doubtful, but Nancy clapped her hands.

"That's capital," she said.

"You know," continued Pennie for the general information, "they burned them."

"Alive?" inquired Ambrose eagerly.

"Yes."

"How jolly!" murmured David.

"Jolly! jolly! jolly!" repeated Dickie, jumping up and down in the snow.

"Why were they burned?" asked Ambrose, who was never tired of asking questions, and liked to get to the bottom of a matter if possible.

"*Why*, I am not quite sure," answered Pennie cautiously, "because I've only just got to it; but I *think* it was something about the Bible. I'll ask Miss Grey."

"Oh, never mind all that," interrupted the practical Nancy impatiently; "we'll make a splendid bonfire all round him and watch him melt. Come and get the wood."

"And we'll call him 'a distinguished martyr,'" added Pennie as she moved slowly away, "because I can't remember any of their real names."

Pennie was never satisfied to leave things as they were; she liked to adorn them with fancies and make up stories about them, and her busy little mind was always ready to set to work on the smallest event of the children's lives. Nothing was too common or familiar to have mysteries and romance woven round it; and this was sometimes a most useful faculty, for winter was not always kind enough to bring snow and ice with him. Very often there was nothing but rain and fog and mud, and then mother uttered those dreadful words:

"The children must not go out."

Then when lessons were over, and all the games exhausted, and it was still too early for lights, the schoolroom became full of dark corners, and the flickering fire cast mysterious shadows which changed the very furniture into something dim and awful.

Then was Pennie's time—then, watching her hearers' upturned faces by the uncertain light of the fire, she saw surprise or pity or horror on them as her story proceeded, and, waxing warmer, she half believed it true herself. And this made the tales very interesting and thrilling. Yet once Pennie's talent had an unfortunate result, as you shall hear in the next chapter.

Chapter Two.

The "Garret."

The children all thought that Pennie's best stories were about a certain lumber-room in the vicarage which was called the "Garret." They were also the most dreadful and thrilling, for there was something about the garret which lent itself readily to tales of mystery and horror. The very air there was always murky and dim, and no sunlight could steal through the tiny lattice window which came poking out from the roof like a half-shut eyelid. Dust and cobwebs had covered the small leaded panes so thickly that a dusky gloom always dwelt there, and gave an unnatural and rather awful look to the various objects. And what a strange collection it was! Broken spindle-legged chairs, rickety boxes, piles of yellow old music-books and manuscripts, and in one corner an ancient harp in a tarnished gilt frame. Poor deserted dusty old things! They had had their day in the busy world once, but that was over now, and they must stay shut up in the silent garret with no one to see them but the spiders and the children. For these last came there often; treading on tiptoe they climbed the steep stairs and unlatched the creaky door and entered, bold but breathless, and casting anxious glances over their shoulders for strange things that might be lurking in the corners. They never saw any, but still they came half hoping, half fearing; and they had, besides, another object in their visits, which was a great great secret, and only known to Pennie, Nancy, and Ambrose. It was indeed a daring adventure, scarcely to be spoken of above a whisper, and requiring a great deal of courage. This was the secret:

They had one day succeeded in forcing open the rickety lattice, which was fastened by a rusty iron hasp, and looked out. There was a steep red-tiled piece of roof covered with little lumps of lichen which ended in a gutter and a low stone balustrade; there were tall crooked chimneys, and plenty of places where cats and children could walk with pleasure and safety. Soon it was impossible to resist the temptation, and one after the other they squeezed themselves through the narrow window, and wriggled cautiously down the steep roof as far as the balustrade. It scraped the hands and knees a good deal to do this, and there was always the danger of going down too fast, but when once the feet arrived safely against the stone coping, what a proud moment it was!

Standing upright, they surveyed the prospect, and mingled visions of Robinson Crusoe, Christopher Columbus, and Alexander Selkirk floated across their brains. "I am monarch of all I survey," said Pennie on the first occasion. And so she was, for everything seen from that giddy height looked strange and new to her, and it was quite like going into another country.

The old church tower with the chattering jackdaws flying round it, the pear-tree near the nursery window, the row of bee-hives in the kitchen-garden, the distant fields where the cows were no bigger than brown and white specks, all were lifted out of everyday life for a little while. No one had forbidden this performance, because no one knew of it, and the secrecy of it added to the mystery which belonged to everything in the garret.

It was not difficult to keep it hidden from the elders, for they did not go into the lumber-room from year's end to year's end; so the spiders and the children had it all to themselves, and did just as they liked there, and wove their cobwebs and their fancies undisturbed. Now, amongst Pennie's listeners when she told her tales of what went on in the garret after nightfall, Ambrose was the one who heard with the most rapt attention and the most absolute belief. He came next to Nancy in age, and formed the most perfect contrast to her in appearance and character, for Nancy was a robust blue-eyed child, bold and fearless, and Ambrose was a slender little fellow with a freckled skin and a face full of sensitive expression. He was full of fears and fancies, too, poor little Ambrose, and amongst the children he was considered not far short of a coward; it had become a habit to say, "Ambrose is afraid," on the smallest occasions, and if they had been asked who was the bravest amongst them, they would certainly have pointed out Nancy. For Nancy did not mind the dark, Nancy would climb any tree you liked, Nancy could walk along the top of a high narrow wall without being giddy, Nancy had never been known to cry when she was hurt, therefore Nancy was a brave child. Ambrose, on the contrary, *did* mind all these things very much; his imagination pictured dangers and terrors in them which did not exist for Nancy, and what she performed with a laugh and no sense of fear, was to him often an occasion of trembling apprehension. And then he was *so* afraid of the dark! That was a special subject of derision from the others, for even Dickie was bolder in the matter of dark passages and bed-rooms than he was. Ambrose was ashamed, bitterly ashamed of this failing, and he made up his mind a hundred times that he would get over it, but that was in the broad daylight when the sun was shining. As surely as night came, and he was asked perhaps to fetch something from the schoolroom, those wretched feelings of fear came back, for the schoolroom was at the end of a long dark passage.

Nancy, who was always good-natured, though she laughed at him, would give him a nudge on such occasions if she were near him, and say:

"Never mind, *I'll* go;" but Ambrose never accepted the offer. He went with a shiver down his back, and a sort of distended feeling in his ears, which seemed to be unnaturally on the alert for mysterious noises.

He always made up his mind before he got to the passage to check a wild desire to run at full speed, and walk through it slowly, but this resolve was never carried out.

Before he had gone two steps in the darkness there would be a sense of something following close behind, and then all was over, and nothing to be seen but a panic-stricken little boy rushing along with his hands held over his ears. How foolish! you will say. Very foolish, indeed, and so said all the other children, adding many a taunt and jeer.

But that did not do poor Ambrose any good, and he remained just as timid as ever. Nevertheless there were moments of real danger when Ambrose had been known to come gallantly to the front, and when he seemed to change suddenly from a fearful, shrinking boy into a hero. Such was the occasion when, alone of all the children, who stood shrieking on the other side of the hedge, he had ventured back into the field to rescue Dickie, who by some accident had been left behind among a herd of cows. There she stood bewildered, holding up her little pinafore full of daisies, helpless among those large horned monsters.

"Run, Dickie," shouted the children; but Dickie was rooted to the ground with terror, and did not move.

Then Ambrose took his courage in both hands, and leaving the safe shelter of the hedge, ran back to his little sister's side. As he reached her a large black cow with crooked horns detached herself from the herd, and walked quickly up to the children lashing her tail. Ambrose did not stir. He stood in front of Dickie, took off his straw hat and waved it in the cow's face. She stood still.

"Run back to the others, Dickie," said Ambrose quietly, and, Dickie's chubby legs recovering power of movement, she toddled quickly off, strewing the ground with daisies as she went. Covering her retreat, Ambrose remained facing the cow, and walked slowly backwards still brandishing his hat; then, one quick glance over his shoulder assuring him of Dickie's safety, he too took to his heels, and scrambled through the gap.

That was certainly brave of Ambrose; for though Farmer Snow told them afterwards, "Thuccy black coo never would a touched 'ee," still she *might* have, and for the moment Ambrose was a hero.

The children carried home an excited account of the affair to their father, penetrating into his very study, which was generally forbidden ground.

"And so it was Ambrose who went back, eh?" he said, stroking Dickie's round head as she sat on his knee.

"Yes, father," said Pennie, very much out of breath with running and talking, "we were all frightened except Ambrose."

"And why weren't you frightened, Ambrose?"

"I was," murmured Ambrose.

"And yet you went?"

"Yes. Because of Dickie."

"Then you were a brave boy."

"A brave boy, a brave boy," repeated Dickie in a sort of sing-song, pulling her father's whiskers.

"Now I want you children to tell me," pursued the vicar, looking round at the hot little eager faces, "which would have been braver—not to be frightened at all, or to go in spite of being frightened?"

"Not to be frightened at all," answered Nancy promptly.

"Do you all think that?"

"Yes," said Pennie doubtfully, "I suppose so."

"Well," continued the vicar, "I *don't* think so, and I will tell you why. I believe the brave man is not he who is insensible to fear, but he who is able to rise above it in doing his duty. People are sometimes called courageous who are really so unimaginative and dull that they cannot understand danger—so of course they are not afraid. They go through their lives very quietly and comfortably, as a rule, but they do not often leave great names behind them, although they may be both good and useful.

"Others, again, we are accustomed to consider cowards, because their active, lively imagination often causes them to see danger where there is none. These people do not pass such peaceable lives as the first; but there is this to be remembered: the same nature which is so alive to fear will also be easily touched by praise, or blame, or ridicule, and eager therefore to do its very best. It is what we call a 'sensitive' nature, and it is of such stuff very often, that great men and heroes are made."

The children listened very attentively to what their father said, and if they did not understand it all they gathered enough to make them feel quite sure that Ambrose had been very brave about the cow. So they treated him for a little while with a certain respect, and no one said "Ambrose is afraid." As for Ambrose himself, his spirits rose very high, and he began to think he never should feel afraid of anything again, and even to wish for some great occasion to show himself in his new character of "hero." He walked about in rather a blustering manner just now, with his straw hat very much on one side, and brandished a stick the gardener had cut for him in an obtrusively warlike fashion. As he was a small thin boy, these airs looked all the more ridiculous, and his sister Nancy was secretly much provoked by them; however, she said nothing until one evening when Pennie was telling them stories.

The children were alone in the schoolroom, for it was holiday time. It was just seven o'clock. Soon Nurse would come and carry off Dickie and David to bed, but at present they were sitting one each side of Pennie on the broad window-seat, listening to her with open ears and mouths. Nancy and Ambrose were opposite on the table, with their legs swinging comfortably backwards and forwards.

All day long it had been raining, and now, although it had ceased, the shrubs and trees, overladen with moisture, kept up a constant drip, drip, drip, which was almost as bad. The wind had risen, and went sighing and moaning round the house, and shook the windows of the room where the children were sitting. Pennie had just finished a story, and in the short interval of silence which followed, these plaintive sounds were heard more plainly than ever.

"Hark," she said, holding up her finger, "how the Goblin Lady is playing her harp to-night! She has begun early."

"Why does she only play when the wind blows?" asked Ambrose.

"She comes *with* the wind," answered Pennie, "that is how she travels, as other people use carriages and trains. The little window in the garret is blown open, and she floats in and takes one of those big music-books, and finds out the place, and then sits down to the harp and plays."

"What tune does she play?" asked David.

"By the margin of fair Zurich's waters," answered Pennie; "sometimes she sings too, but not often, because she is very sad."

"Why?" inquired Ambrose, ruffling up his hair with one hand, as he always did when he was getting interested.

Pennie paused a moment that her next remark might have full weight; then very impressively and slowly she said:

"She has not *always* been a Goblin Lady."

This was so unexpected, and suggested so much to be unfolded, that the children gazed speechless at Pennie, who presently continued:

"Once she was a beautiful—"

"Is she ugly now?" hastily inquired David.

"Don't, Davie; let Pennie go on," said Ambrose.

"I want to know just one thing," put in Nancy; "if it's dark when she comes, how does she see to read the music?"

"She carries glowworms with her," answered Pennie; "they shine just like the lamps in father's gig at night, and light up all the garret."

"Now, go on, Pennie," said Ambrose with a deep sigh, for these interruptions were very trying to him. "Once she was a beautiful—"

"A most beautiful lady, with long golden hair. Only she was very very proud and vain. So after she died she could not rest, but has to go flying about wherever the wind will take her. The only pleasure she has is music, and so she always tries to get in where there is anything to play. That is why she goes so often to the garret and plays the harp."

"Why doesn't she go into the drawing-room and play the piano?" asked Nancy bluntly. Nancy's questions were often very tiresome; she never allowed the least haze or uncertainty to hang over any subject, and Pennie was frequently checked in the full flow of her eloquence by the consciousness that Nancy's eye was upon her, and that she was preparing to put some matter-of-fact inquiry which it would be most difficult to meet.

"There you go, interrupting again," muttered Ambrose.

"Well, but why doesn't she?" insisted Nancy, "it would be so much easier."

"Why, of course she can't," resumed Pennie in rather an injured voice, "because of the lights, and the people, and, besides, she never learnt to play the piano."

"I wish I needn't either," sighed Nancy. "How nice to be like the Goblin Lady, and only play the harp when one likes!"

"I should like to see her," said Ambrose thoughtfully.

"You'd be afraid," said Nancy; "why, you wouldn't even go into the garret by daylight alone."

"That was a long time ago," said Ambrose quickly. "I wouldn't mind it now."

"In the dark?"

"Well, I don't believe you'd go," said Nancy. "You might perhaps go two or three steps, and then you'd scream out and run away; wouldn't he, Pennie?"

"Why, you know he *was* brave about the cow," said Pennie, "braver than any of us."

"That was different. He's quite as much afraid of the dark as ever. I call it babyish."

Nancy looked defiantly at her brother, who was getting very red in the face. She was prepared to have something thrown at her, or at least to have her hair, which she wore in a plaited pig-tail, violently pulled, but nothing of the sort happened. Nurse came soon afterwards and bore away David and Dickie, and as she left the room she remarked that the wind was moaning "just like a Christian."

It certainly was making a most mournful noise that evening, but not at all like a Christian, Ambrose thought, as he listened to it—much more like Pennie's Goblin Lady and her musical performances.

Pennie had finished her stories now, and she and Nancy were deeply engaged with their dolls in a corner of the room; this being an amusement in which Ambrose took no interest, he remained seated on the table occupied with his own reflections after Nurse had left the room with the two children.

Nancy's taunt about the garret was rankling in his mind, though he had not resented it openly as was his custom, and it rankled all the more because he felt that it was true. Yes, it *was* true. He could not possibly go into the garret alone in the dark, and yet if he really were a brave boy he ought to be able to do it. Was he brave, he wondered? Father had said so, and yet just now he certainly felt something very like fear at the very thought of the Goblin Lady.

In increasing perplexity he ruffled up his hair until it stood out wildly in all directions; boom! boom! went the wind, and then there followed a long wailing sort of sigh which seemed to come floating down from the very top of the house.

It was quite a relief to hear Nancy's matter-of-fact voice just then, as she chattered away about her dolls:

"Now, I shall brush Jemima's hair," Ambrose heard her say to Pennie, "and you can put Lady Jane Grey to bed."

"I ought to be able to go," said Ambrose to himself, "and after all I don't suppose the Goblin Lady *can* be worse than Farmer Snow's black cow."

"But her head's almost off," put in Pennie's voice. "You did it the last time we executed her."

"If I went," thought Ambrose, continuing his reflections, "they would never, never be able to call me a coward again."

He slid off the table as he reached this point, and moved slowly towards the door. He stood still as he opened it and looked at his sisters, half hoping they would call him back, or ask where he was going, but they were bending absorbed over the body of the unfortunate Lady Jane Grey, so that two long flaxen pig-tails were turned towards him. They did not even notice that he had moved.

He went quickly through the long dimly-lighted passage, which led into the hall, and found that Mary was just lighting the lamp. This looked cheerful, and he lingered a little and asked her a few questions, not that he really wanted to know anything, but because light and human companionship seemed just now so very desirable. Mary went away soon, and then he strolled a few steps up the broad old staircase, and met Kittles the fluffy cat coming slowly down. Here was another excuse for putting off his journey, and he sat down on the stairs to pass a few agreeable moments with Kittles, who arched his back and butted his head against him, and purred his acknowledgments loudly. But presently, having business of his own, Kittles also passed on his way, and Ambrose was alone again, sitting solitary with his ruffled head leaning on one hand. Then the church clock struck eight. In half an hour it would be bed-time, and his plan not carried out. He must go at once, or not at all. He got up and went slowly on. Up the stairs, down a long winding passage, up some more stairs, and across a landing, on to which the nursery and the children's bedrooms opened. He stopped again here, for there was a pleasant sound of Dickie and David's voices, and the splashing of water; but presently he thought he heard Nurse coming out, and he ran quickly round the corner into a little passage which led to the foot of the garret stairs. This passage was dimly-lighted by a small low window, which was almost covered outside by the thickly growing ivy. Even in the daytime it was very dusky, and now it was quite dark, but Ambrose knew the way well, and he groped about with his hands until he came to the steep carpetless steps. And now his heart began to beat very quickly, for he felt that he was in the region of mystery, and that anything might happen at any moment. The wind had dropped, and there was no sound at all to be heard, though he strained his ears to the utmost for some signs of the presence of the Goblin Lady.

"Perhaps," thought he, "she has finished playing and gone away again with the wind." This was an encouraging idea, and though his knees trembled a good deal, he went on bravely until he came to the place where the stairs took a sudden sharp turn; but here he saw something which brought him to a standstill again, for underneath the garret door at the top there was a faint gleam of light. "That's the glowworms," thought Ambrose, "and she's there still." His spirits sank.

Could he go on? It must be now or never. With a tremendous effort he went quickly up the remaining steps, stood on tiptoe to unlatch the door, and pushed it open. It swung back with a creak upon its rusty hinges, and a cold wind rushed in Ambrose's face, for the window was open. The room was faintly lighted, not with glowworms, but by the pale rays of a watery moon, which made some of the objects whitely distinct, and left others dark and shadowy. Standing motionless on the threshold, Ambrose turned his eyes instinctively to the corner where the harp was dimly visible. There was certainly no one playing it, but as he looked he heard a faint rustle in that direction. What was it? Again it came, this time louder, with a sound like the flapping of feathers. Could it be the Goblin Lady? But Pennie never said she had wings. Unable to go either backwards or forwards, Ambrose remained rooted to the spot with his eyes fixed on the mysterious corner. Rustle, rustle, flap, flap, went the dreadful something, and presently there followed a sort of low hiss. At the same moment a sudden gust of wind burst through the window and banged the door behind him with a resounding clap. Panic-stricken he turned and tried to open it, but his cold trembling fingers could not move the rusty fastening. He looked wildly round for a means of escape, and his eye fell on a bright ray of moonlight resting on the lattice window. He rushed towards it, scrambled up on to a box, from thence to the window-ledge, and thrust himself through the narrow opening. If the thing came after him now, he could go no further than the balustrade, unless he jumped down into the garden, "and that would kill me," he thought, "Pennie has often said so."

He stood on the rough tiles, holding on to the iron window frame with one hand; behind him the dark garret, where the thing still flapped and rustled, and before him the sloping roof, the tall chimneys, the garden beneath, partly lighted up by the moon. He could see the nursery window, too, in an angle of the house, brightly illumined by the cheerful fire within. Dickie and David were snugly in bed now, warm and safe, and Nurse was most likely searching everywhere for him. If they only knew!

"If ever I get back," he said to himself, "I never *will* try to be brave again; it's much better to be called a coward always." He had hardly come to this conclusion before, with a tremendous whirring noise, something came banging up against the shut part of the window from within the garret. Ambrose gave one wild scream, let go his hold, and went rolling over and over quicker and quicker, down—down—down.

Chapter Three.
Goblinet.

He remembered nothing more until he woke up that night in his own little bed with a very confused feeling that something dreadful had happened, though he could not think what it was. There was a light in his room, which was strange too, and presently he saw that Nurse was sitting there with her spectacles on, nodding sleepily over a book. What could it mean? He clasped his head with both hands, and tried to remember; but it was startling to find that there was a wet bandage round it, and inside it there was a dull throbbing ache, so he soon gave up trying and lay quietly with his eyes fixed on Nurse, and the funny shadow she made on the wall. At last she gave a most tremendous nod, which knocked off her spectacles, and then she gathered herself up and opened her eyes very wide. Presently she came to the bed with a glass in her hand and leant over Ambrose to see if he was awake; he drank what she gave him eagerly, for he was thirsty, and as he lay down again he said with an effort:

"I think I've had a very bad dream, Nurse, and my head *does* ache so."

"Well, you're safe and sound now, my lamb," she answered, patting his shoulder soothingly; "just you turn round and go to sleep again."

Still puzzled Ambrose closed his eyes, and wondered vaguely for a few minutes why Nurse called him "lamb." She had not done it since he had the measles, so he supposed he must be ill; but he did not feel at all equal to asking questions about anything, and was soon fast asleep again.

But this was the beginning of many weary days and nights for poor little Ambrose. When the doctor came the next day he looked gravely at Mrs Hawthorn.

"The child is in a high fever," he said, "and has had, I should think, some great nervous shock. Great care and quiet are needed. Let him sleep as much as possible."

But that was the difficulty, for, as time went on, Ambrose seemed less and less able to sleep quietly at night. As evening drew on the fever and restlessness increased; he could not bear to be left alone a moment, and often in the night he would start up and cry out trembling:

"Take her away." "She is coming." "Don't let her catch me."

It was most distressing for everyone and puzzling too, for no one could imagine what it was that had frightened him in the garret, or how he came to be there at all at that time in the evening. It was evidently a most terrible remembrance to him, for he could not bear the least reference to it, and to question him was a sure way to give him what he called "bad dreams." So in his presence the subject was dropped; but Mrs Hawthorn and Nurse did not cease their conjectures, and there was one person who listened to their conversation with a feeling of the deepest guilt. This was Pennie, who just now was having a most miserable time of it, for she felt that it was all her fault. If she had not told those stories about the Goblin Lady it never would have happened, although it certainly was Nancy who had put the garret into Ambrose's head.

Nancy was the only person she could talk to on the subject, but she was not any comfort at all.

"Don't let's think about it," she said. "I knew you made it up. I daresay he'll get better soon."

Poor Pennie could not take matters so lightly; it was a most dreadful weight on her mind, and she felt sure she should never have another happy minute till she had confessed about the

Goblin Lady. But she was not allowed to see Ambrose, and she could not bring herself to tell anyone else about it. Once she nearly told mother, and then something stuck in her throat; and once she got as far as the study door with the intention of telling father, but her courage failed her and she ran away.

She would creep to Ambrose's door and listen, or peep round the screen at him while he was asleep, and her face got quite thin and pointed with anxiety. Every morning she asked:

"Is he better, mother? May I go and sit with him?" But the answer always was:

"Not to-day, dear. We hope he is better, but he has such bad nights."

Pennie was very wretched, and felt she could not bear it much longer.

She was in the nursery one morning looking listlessly out of the window, when her attention was caught by a conversation going on between Nurse and Mrs Hawthorn, who was sitting there with Cicely in her arms.

"I know no more than that baby, ma'am," said Nurse emphatically, as she had said a hundred times before, "why or wherefore Master Ambrose should take such a thing into his head. It's easy to frame that he should get scared—when once he was up there in the dark, for he's a timid child and always has been. But what *took* him there all alone? That's what *I* want to know!"

"I cannot understand it," said Mrs Hawthorn; "but it makes him so much worse to ask him questions that we must leave it alone until he is stronger. We cannot be too thankful that he was not killed."

"Which I never doubted for one moment that he was, ma'am, when I found him," continued Nurse; "he was lying all crumpled up and stone-cold, for all the world like Miss Nancy's dormouse when she forgot to feed it for a week."

On this theme Nurse was apt to become very voluble, and there were few things she liked better than describing her own feelings on the occasion. Mrs Hawthorn held up her hand entreatingly: "Do not talk of it, Nurse," she said; "I cannot bear it." And then they went on to discuss other matters.

Now all this while Pennie had been trying to make up her mind to speak. There was a fly just in front of her on the window-pane, and as she watched it crawling slowly along she said to herself:

"When it gets as far as the corner I will tell mother." But alas! before the fly had nearly completed his journey Mrs Hawthorn rose to leave the nursery. As she passed Pennie she stopped and said:

"Why, Pennie, my child, it is not like you to be idle. And you look mournful; what's the matter?"

"I think Miss Pennie frets after her brother, ma'am," observed Nurse.

"Well, then," said Mrs Hawthorn, "I have something to tell you that I am sure you will like. The doctor thinks Ambrose much better to-day, and if you are very quiet and discreet I will let you go and have tea with him this afternoon at five o'clock."

"Oh, mother, mother," cried Pennie, "how lovely! May I really?"

"Yes; but you must promise me one thing, and that is that you will not speak of anything that has to do with the garret or his accident."

Pennie's face fell.

"Very well, mother," she said in a dejected tone.

"If you can't feel sure, Pennie," said her mother observing

the hesitation, "I can't let you go."

"I won't, really, mother," repeated Pennie with a sigh — "truly and faithfully."

But she felt almost as low-spirited as ever, for what was the good of seeing Ambrose if she could not make him understand about the Goblin Lady? She remained at the window pondering the subject, with her eyes fixed on the grey church tower, the top of which she could just see through the branches of the pear-tree. It reminded her somehow of her father's text last Sunday, and how pleased she and Nancy had been because it was such a short one to learn. Only two words: "Pray always." She said it to herself now over and over again without thinking much about it, until it suddenly struck her that it would be a good thing to say a little prayer and ask to be helped out of the present difficulty. "If I believe enough," she said to herself, "I shall be helped. Father says people always are helped if they believe enough when they ask."

She shut her eyes up very tight and repeated earnestly several times: "I *do* believe. I really and truly do believe;" and then she said her prayer.

After this she felt a little more comfortable and ran out to play with Nancy, firmly believing that before five o'clock something would turn up to her assistance.

But Pennie was doomed to disappointment, for five o'clock came without any way out of the difficulty having presented itself.

"I suppose I didn't believe hard enough," she said to herself as she made her way sorrowfully upstairs to Ambrose's room. Just as she thought this the study door opened and her father came out. He was carrying something which looked like a large cage covered with a cloth. Pennie stopped and waited till he came up to her.

"Why, whatever can that be, father?" she said. "Is it alive? Where are you taking it?"

"It is a little visitor for Ambrose," he answered; "and I'm taking him upstairs to tea with you both. But you're not to look at him yet;" for Pennie was trying to peep under the cloth.

When they got into Ambrose's room she was relieved to find that he looked just like himself, though his face was very white and thin. He was much better to-day, and able to sit up in a big arm-chair with a picture-book. But nevertheless before Nurse left the room she whispered to Pennie again that she must be very quiet.

There was no need for the caution at present, for Pennie was in one of her most subdued moods, though at any other time she would have been very much excited to know what was inside the cage.

"Now," said the vicar when he was seated in the arm-chair, with Ambrose settled comfortably on his knee, "we shall see what Ambrose and this little gentleman have to say to each other."

He lifted off the covering, and there was the dearest little brown and white owl in the world, sitting winking and blinking in the sudden light.

Ambrose clasped his little thin hands, and his eyes sparkled with pleasure.

"Oh, father," he cried, "what a darling dear! Is he for me? I always *did* want to have an owl so!"

He was in such raptures when he was told that the owl was to be his very own, that when the tea was brought in he could hardly be persuaded to touch it. Pennie, too, almost forgot her troubles in the excitement of pouring out tea, and settling with Ambrose where the owl was to live.

"The nicest place will be," at last said Ambrose decidedly, "in that corner of the barn just above where Davie's rabbits are. You know, Pennie. Where it's all dusky, and dark, and cobwebby."

"I think that sounds just the sort of place he would feel at home in," said their father; "and now, would you like me to tell you where I got him?"

"Oh, yes, please, father," said Ambrose, letting his head drop on Mr Hawthorn's shoulder with a deep sigh of contentment. "Tell us every little scrap about it, and don't miss any."

"Well, last night, about nine o'clock, when I was writing in the study, I wanted to refer to an old book of sermons, and I couldn't remember where it was. I looked all over my book-cases, and at last I went and asked mother, and she told me that it was most likely put away in the garret."

Ambrose stirred uneasily, and Pennie thought to herself, "They said I wasn't to mention the garret, and here's father talking about it like anything."

"So I took a lamp," continued Mr Hawthorn, "and went upstairs, and poked about in the garret a long while. I found all sorts of funny old things there, but not the book I wanted, so I was just going down again when I heard a rustling in one corner —"

Pennie could see that Ambrose's eyes were very wide open, with a terrified stare as if he saw something dreadful, and he was clinging tightly with one hand to his father's coat.

"So I went into the corner and moved away a harp which was standing there, and what do you think I saw? This little fluffy gentleman just waked up from a nap, and making a great fuss and flapping. He was very angry when I caught him, and hissed and scratched tremendously; but I said, 'No, my friend, I cannot let you go. You will just do for my little son, Ambrose.' So I put him into a basket for the night, and this morning I got a cage for him in the village, and here he is."

Mr Hawthorn looked down at Ambrose as he finished his story: the frightened expression which Pennie had seen had left the boy's face now, and there was one of intense relief there. He folded his hands, and said softly, drawing a deep breath:

"Then it was not the Goblin Lady after all."

"The Goblin Lady! What can the child mean?" said the vicar looking inquiringly at Pennie.

But he got no answer to his question, for Pennie's long-pent-up feelings burst forth at last. Casting discretion to the winds, she threw her arms vehemently round Ambrose, and blurted out half laughing and half crying:

"I made it up! I made it up! There *isn't* any Goblin Lady. Oh, dear! Oh, dear! I made it every bit up!"

The two children sobbed and laughed and kissed each other, and made incoherent exclamations in a way which their puzzled father felt to be most undesirable for an invalid's room. He had been carefully warned not to excite Ambrose, and what *could* be worse than this sort of thing?

Perfectly bewildered, he said sternly:

"Pennie, if you don't command yourself, you must go out of the room. You will make your brother ill. It is most thoughtless of you. Tell me quietly what all this means."

With many jerks and interruptions, and much shamefacedness Pennie proceeded to do so. Looking up at her father's face at the end she was much relieved to see a little smile there, though he did not speak at once.

"You're not angry, are you, father?" said Ambrose doubtfully at last.

"No, I am not angry," replied Mr Hawthorn, "but I am certainly surprised to find I have two such foolish children. I don't know who was the sillier—Pennie to make up such nonsense, or Ambrose to believe it. But now I am not going to say anything more, because it is quite time for Ambrose to go to bed, so Pennie and the owl and I will say good-night."

What a relief it was to hear the dreaded subject spoken of so lightly. Pennie felt as though a great heavy weight had been suddenly lifted off her mind, and she was so glad and happy that after she had left Ambrose's room she could not possibly walk along quietly. So she hopped on one leg all down a long passage, and at the top of the stairs she met Nurse hastening up to her patient:

"You look merry, Miss Pennie," said she. "I hope you haven't been exciting Master Ambrose."

"Why, yes," Pennie couldn't help answering. "Father and I have both excited him a good deal; but he's much better, and now he'll get quite well."

And Pennie was right, for from that night Ambrose improved steadily, though it was some time before he became quite strong and lost his nervous fears.

The first visit he paid, when he was well enough to be wheeled into the garden in a bath-chair, escorted by the triumphant children, was to see his new pet, the owl. There he was, hanging in his cage in the darkest corner of the barn. Ambrose looked up at him with eyes full of the fondest affection.

"What shall we call him, Pennie?" he said. "I want some name which has to do with a goblin."

Pennie considered the subject with her deepest frown.

"Would 'Goblinet' do?" she said at length; "because, you see, he is so small."

"Beautifully," said Ambrose.

So the owl was called "Goblinet."

Chapter Four.

David's Pig.

By the time Ambrose was quite well again, and able to run about with the others and play as usual, the holidays were over; Miss Grey came back, and lessons began.

It was late autumn; hay-time had passed and harvest, and all the fields looked brown and bare and stubbly. The garden paths were covered with dry withered leaves, which made a pleasant sound when you shuffled your feet in them, and were good things for Dickie to put into her little barrow, for as often as she collected them there were soon plenty more. Down they came from the trees, red, brown, yellow, when the wind blew, and defied the best efforts of Dickie and Andrew. There were very few flowers left now—only a few dahlias and marigolds, and some clumps of Michaelmas daisies, so the garden looked rather dreary; but to make up for this there was a splendid crop of apples in the orchard, and the lanes were thickly strewn with bright brown acorns. And these last were specially interesting to David, for it was just about this time that he got his pig.

David was a solid squarely-built little boy of seven years old, with hair so light that it looked almost grey, and very solemn blue eyes. He spoke seldom, and took a long time to learn things, but when once that was done he never forgot them; and in this he was unlike Nancy, who could learn quickly, but forget almost as soon. Miss Grey always felt sure that when once David had struggled through a lesson, whether it were the kings and queens of England, or the multiplication table, that he would remember it if she asked him a question weeks afterwards. But then it was a long time before he knew it—so long that it often seemed a hopeless task. Nevertheless, if David was slow he was certainly sure, and people had a habit of depending upon him in various matters. For instance, when Nurse wanted to intrust the baby for a few moments to any of the children during her absence from the nursery, it was never to the three elder she turned, but to David, and her confidence was not misplaced. Once having undertaken any charge or responsibility, David would carry it through unflinchingly, whether it were to amuse the baby, or to take care of any of the animals while their various owners were away. It would have been impossible to him to have forgotten to feed the dormouse for a week as Nancy did, or to have left Sappho the canary without any water, which Pennie to her great agony of mind was once guilty of doing.

David's animals never missed their meals, or were neglected in any way; he was particularly proud of his sleek rabbits, which, together with a family of white rats, lived in the barn, and certainly throve wonderfully, if numbers mean prosperity. The biggest rabbit was called Goliath, and it was David's delight to hold him up by the ears, in spite of his very powerful kicks, and exhibit his splendid condition to any admiring beholder. But though Goliath was handsome, and the white rats numerous, their owner was not quite satisfied, for his fondest wish for some time past had been to possess a pig. A nice little round black pig, with a very curly tail; he would then be content, and ask nothing further of fortune.

He thought of the pig, and hoped for the pig, and it would not be too much to say that he dreamed of the pig. When he passed a drove of them in the road, squeaking, pushing, grunting, and going every way but the right, he would stand in speechless admiration. His mind was a practical one, and did not dwell merely on the pleasure of owning the pig itself, but also on the prospect of fattening, selling, and realising money by it.

"You'd never be able to have it killed," said Nancy, who

was his chief confidante, "after you got fond of it, and it got to know you; you'd as soon kill Goliath."

"I shouldn't have it killed," answered David. "I should sell it to the farmer."

"Well; but *he'd* have it killed," pursued the relentless Nancy.

This was unanswerable.

"Never mind. I want a pig, and I shall save up my money," said David sturdily.

David's bank was a white china house which stood on the nursery mantel-shelf; it had a very red roof with a hole in it, and into this he continued for some time to drop all his pennies, and halfpennies, and farthings with great persistency, and a mind steadily fixed on the pig. After all, however, he got it without spending any of his savings, and this is how it happened: —

One fine morning at the end of September the children were all ready for their usual walk with Miss Grey—all, that is, except Dickie, who, being still a nursery child, went out walking with Nurse and baby. The other four, however, were ready, not only as regards hats and jackets, but were also each provided with something to "take out," which, in their opinion, was quite as indispensable. Penelope therefore carried a sketching book, Ambrose a boat under one arm, and under the other a camp-stool in case Miss Grey should be tired, Nancy two dolls and a skipping-rope, and David a whip and a long chain. At the end of this was the terrier dog Snuff, choking and struggling with excitement, and giving vent to smothered barks. Snuff would willingly have been loose, and there was indeed not the least occasion for this restraint, as it would have been far easier to lose David than the dog; he knew well, however, that children have their little weaknesses in these matters, and submitted to his bondage with only a few whines of remonstrance when the company had once fairly started.

His patience was a good deal tried on this occasion, as well as that of the children, for it seemed as though Mrs Hawthorn never would finish talking to Miss Grey in the hall. At last, however, she said something which pleased them very much:

"I want you to go to Hatchard's Farm for me, and ask about the butter."

Now Hatchard's Farm was the place of all others that the children delighted to visit. It was about two miles from Easney, and the nicest way to it was across some fields, where you could find mushrooms, into a little narrow lane where the thickly growing blackberry brambles caught and scratched at you as you passed. This lane was muddy in winter, and at no time in the year did it appear so desirable to Miss Grey as to the children; but it was such a favourite walk with them that she generally yielded. The only other way of getting to the farm was by the high-road, and that was so dreadfully dull! After scrambling along the lane a little while, you saw the red-brown roofs of the barns and outbuildings clustering round the house itself, and almost hiding it, and soon a pleasant confusion of noises met your ear. Ducks quacked, hens cackled, pigeons perched about on the roofs kept up a monotonous murmur; then came the deep undertones of the patient cows, and as you neared the house you could generally hear Mrs Hatchard's voice in her dairy adding its commanding accents to the medley of sounds. It certainly was a delightful farm, and David had long ago determined that when he grew up he would have one just like it, and wear brown leather gaiters like Farmer Hatchard's. He would also keep pigs like his—quite black, with very short legs and faces, and tightly curled tails. But some time must pass before this, and the next best thing was to go as often as possible to see them, and ask all manner of questions of the farmer or his men. There was no one in the great wide kitchen when the party arrived on this occasion, and Miss Grey sat down to wait for Mrs Hatchard, while the children made their usual tour of admiring examination. They had seen every object in the room hundreds of times before, but how interesting they always were! The high-backed settle on each side of the fire was dark with age, and bright with the toil of Mrs Hatchard's hands; the heavy oak rafters were so conveniently low that the children could see the farmer's gun, a bunch of dips, a pair of clogs, a side of bacon kept there as in a sort of storehouse. At the end of the room opposite the wide hearth was the long narrow deal table, where the farmer and his men all dined together at twelve o'clock, for they were old-fashioned people at Hatchard's Farm; and behind the door hung the cuckoo clock, before which the children never failed to stand in open-mouthed expectation if it were near striking the hour. On all this the sun darted his rays through the low casement, and failed to find, for all his keen glances, one speck of dust.

Miss Grey sat in the window-seat looking absently out at the marigolds and asters in the gay garden, when she felt a little hand suddenly placed in hers, and, turning round, saw David, his face crimson with suppressed excitement:

"Come," he said, pulling her gently, "come and look here."

He led her to the hearth, and pointed speechless to something which looked like a small flannel bundle in a basket. As she looked at it, it moved a little.

"Well, Davie," said she, "what is this wonderful thing? Something alive?"

David had knelt down close to the bundle and was peering in between the folds of the flannel with an expression of reverent awe. He looked up gravely.

"Don't you see," he said slowly in lowered accents, "it's a little baby pig!"

Stooping down Miss Grey examined it more closely, and found that it was indeed a little black pig of very tender age, so closely covered up in flannel that only its small pointed snout and one eye were visible.

"Do you suppose it's ill?" inquired David.

"I daresay it is," answered Miss Grey; "we'll ask Mrs Hatchard about it presently."

The other children had gathered round, all more or less interested in the invalid pig; but presently, Pennie having suggested that they should go and see the new little calf, they ran out of the kitchen in search of fresh excitement.

"Come along, Davie," said Ambrose, looking back from the door; "come out and see the other pigs."

"No," said David decidedly, "I shall stop here."

He took his seat as he spoke on the corner of the settle nearest the pig, with the evident intention of waiting for Mrs Hatchard's arrival; he was not going to lose a chance of inquiring closely into such an important subject.

And at last Mrs Hatchard came bustling in, cheerful, brisk, and ruddy-faced as usual, with many apologies for her delay. Miss Grey plunged at once into business with her, and the patient David sat silently biding his time for the fit moment to put his questions.

"Won't you run out, little master?" said the good-natured farmer's wife, noticing the grave little figure at last. "There's the calves to see, and a fine litter of likely young pigs too."

"No, thank you," said David politely. "I want to know, please, why you keep this one little pig in here, and whether it's ill."

"Oh, aye," said Mrs Hatchard, coming up to the basket and stooping to look at the occupant, which was now making a feeble grunting noise. "I'd most forgot it. You see it's the Antony pig, and it's that weakly and dillicut I took it away to give it a chance. I doubt I sha'n't rear it, though, for it seems a poor little morsel of a thing."

"How many other little pigs are there?" asked David.

"Why, there's ten on 'em—all fine likely pigs except this one, and they do that push and struggle and fight there's no chance for him."

"Why do you call it the Antony pig?" pursued David with breathless interest.

"Well, I don't rightly know why or wherefore," said Mrs Hatchard; "it's just a name the folks about here always give to the smallest pig in the litter."

"Do you think Farmer Hatchard knows?" inquired David.

"Well, he might," said Mrs Hatchard, "and then again he mightn't. But I tell you what, Master David, if yonder little pig lives, and providin' the vicar has no objections, I'll give him to you. You always fancied pigs, didn't you now?"

David was still leaning fondly over the basket, and made no reply at first. It took some time to fully understand the reality of such a splendid offer.

"Come, Davie," said Miss Grey, "we must say good-bye and go and find the others."

Then he got up, and held out his hand gravely to Mrs Hatchard.

"Good-bye," he said. "Thank you. I hope you'll accede in rearing the Antony pig. I should like to have it very much, if father will let me."

David went home from the farm hardly able to believe in his own good fortune, but according to his custom he said very little.

The matter was discussed freely, however, by the other children, and it was so interesting that it lasted them all the way back. Would the pig live? they wondered, and if it did, would their father let David have it? Where would it live? What would David call the pig if he did get it? This last inquiry was put by Ambrose, and he felt quite rebuked when his brother replied scornfully, "Antony, of course."

But there was some demur on the part of the vicar when he was informed of the proposed addition to his live stock.

"I don't like to disappoint you, my boy," he said, "but you know Andrew has plenty to do already. He has the garden to look after, and the cows, and my horse. I don't think I could ask him to undertake anything more."

Poor little David's face fell, and his underlip was pushed out piteously. He would not have cried for the world, and none of the children ever thought of questioning what their father said; so he stood silent, though he felt that the world without the Antony pig would be empty indeed.

"Do you want it very much, Davie?" said the vicar, looking up from his writing at the mournful little face.

"Yes, father, I do," said David, and with all his resolution he could not choke back a little catching sob as he spoke.

"Well, then, look here," said his father; "if you will promise me to take entire charge of it, and never to trouble Andrew, or call him away from his work to attend to it, you shall have the pig. But if I find that it is neglected in any way, I shall send it back at once to Farmer Hatchard. Is that a bargain?"

"Oh, yes, indeed," cried the delighted David; and he ran out to tell the result of his interview to the anxious children waiting outside the study door.

So David was to have the pig; and, with the assistance of Ambrose and a few words of advice from Andrew, he at once began to prepare a habitation for it. Fortunately there was an old sty still in existence, which only wanted a little repairing, and everything was soon ready. But the rearing of the Antony pig still hung trembling in the balance, and some anxious weeks were passed by David; he called to inquire after it as often as he possibly could, and, to his great joy, found it on each occasion more lively and thriving—thanks to Mrs Hatchard's devoted care.

And at last the long-wished-for day arrived. Antony was driven to his new home with a string tied round his leg, in the midst of a triumphal procession of children, and David's joy and exultation were complete.

There was certainly no danger of his neglecting his charge, or of asking anyone to assist him in its service; never was pig so well cared for as Antony, and as time went on he showed an intelligent appreciation of David's attentions not unmixed with affection. Perhaps in consequence of these attentions he soon developed much shrewdness of character, and had many little humorous ways which were the pride of his master's heart. The two were fast friends, and seemed to understand each other without the need of speech, though David had been known to talk to his pig when he believed himself to be in private. As for the *selling* part of the plan, it seemed quite to have faded away, and when Andrew said with a grin:

"Well, young master, t'pig 'ull soon be ready for market noo," David got quite hot and angry, and changed the subject at once.

On rare occasions Antony was conducted, making unctuous snorts of pleasure, into the field to taste a little fresh grass and rout about with his inquisitive nose; but the garden was of course forbidden ground. Therefore, when he was once discovered in the act of enjoying himself amongst Andrew's potatoes, the consternation was extreme. It was Nancy who saw him, as she sat one morning learning a French verb, and staring meanwhile absently out of the schoolroom window. Her expression changed suddenly from utter vacancy to keen interest, and her monotonous murmur of "J'ai, Tu as, Il a," to a shout of, "Oh, Davie, there's Antony in the garden!"

"Nancy," said Miss Grey severely, "you know it is against rules to talk in lesson time. Be quiet."

"But I can't really, Miss Grey," said Nancy, craning her neck to get a better view of the culprit; "he's poking up the potatoes like anything. Andrew *will* be so cross. You'd better just let us go and chase him back again."

The excitement had now risen so high that Miss Grey felt this would really be the best plan, for attention to lessons seemed impossible, and soon the four children were rushing helter-skelter across the garden in pursuit of Antony. With a frisk of his tail and a squeak of defiance he led the chase in fine style, choosing Andrew's most cherished borders. What a refreshment it was, after the tedium of French verbs and English history, and what a pity when Antony, after a brave resistance, was at length hustled back into his sty!

Whether the door was insecure, or not too carefully fastened after this, remains uncertain; but it is a fact that these pig-chases came to be of pretty frequent occurrence, and always happened, by some strange chance, during school hours. The cry of, "Pig out!" and the consequent rush of children in pursuit, at last reached such a pitch that both Miss Grey and the much-tried Andrew made complaint to the vicar. Miss Grey declared that discipline was becoming impossible, and Andrew that there would not be a "martal vegetable in the garden if Master David's pig got out so often." Then the vicar made a rule to this effect:

"If David's pig is seen in the garden again, it goes back that same day to Farmer Hatchard."

The vicar's rules were not things to be disregarded, and his threats were always carried out. David and Ambrose might have been seen with a large hammer and nails very busy at the pig-sty that afternoon, and Antony's visits to the garden ceased, until one unlucky occasion when David was away from home, and it fell out in the following manner:—

In the cathedral town of Nearminster, ten miles from Easney, lived Pennie's godmother Miss Unity Cheffins, and it was Mr and Mrs Hawthorn's custom to pay her an annual visit of two or three days, taking each of the four elder children with them in turn. It was an occasion much anticipated by the latter, but more for the honour of the thing than from any actual pleasure connected with it, for Miss Unity was rather a stiff old lady, and particular in her notions as to their proper behaviour. She was fond of saying, "In *my* time young people did so and so," and of noticing any little failure in politeness, or even any personal defect. She was a rich old lady, and lived in a great square house just inside the Cathedral Close; it was sombrely furnished, and full of dark old portraits, and rare china bowls and knick-knacks, which last Miss Unity thought a great deal of, and dusted carefully with her own hands. Amongst the many injunctions impressed upon the children, they were told never to touch the china, and there were indeed so many pitfalls to be avoided, that the visit was not by any means an unmixed pleasure to Mrs Hawthorn. The children themselves, however, though they missed the freedom of their home, and were a little afraid of the upright Miss Unity, managed to extract enjoyment from it, and always looked enviously upon the one of their number whose turn it was to go to Nearminster.

And now the time had come round again, and it was David's turn to go, but there was one drawback to his pleasure, because he must leave the pig. Who could say that some careless hand might not leave the door of the sty open or insecurely fastened during his absence? Then Antony's fate would be certain, for Andrew was only too eager to carry out the vicar's sentence of banishment, and was on the watch for the least excuse to hurry the pig back to the farm.

After turning it over in his mind, David came to the conclusion that he could best ensure Antony's safety by placing him under someone's special care, and he chose Nancy for this important office.

"You *will* take care of him, won't you?" he said, drawing up very close to her and fixing earnest eyes upon her face, "and see that his gate is always fastened."

Nancy was deeply engaged in painting a picture in the *Pilgrim's Progress*; she paused a moment to survey the effect of Apollyon in delicate sea-green, and said rather absently:

"Of course I will. And so will Ambrose and so will Pennie."

"No, but I want you partickerlerlery to do it," said David, bungling dreadfully over the long word in his anxiety —"you *more* than the others."

"All right," said Nancy with her head critically on one side.

"I want you to promise three things," went on David —"to keep his gate shut, and to give him acorns, and not to let Dickie poke a stick at him."

"Oh, yes, I'll promise," said Nancy readily.

"Truly and faithfully?" continued David, edging still closer up to her; "you won't forget?"

"No, I really won't," said Nancy with an impatient jerk of her elbow; "don't you worry me any more about it."

"I took care of your dormouse when *you* went," continued David, "and didn't forget it once. So you ought to take care of my pig, it's only fair."

"Well, don't I tell you I'm going to?" said Nancy, laying down her paint-brush with an air of desperation. "I sha'n't do it a bit more for your asking so often. Do leave off."

"You'll only be away three days, Davie," said Pennie, looking up from her book; "we can manage to take care of Antony that little while I should think."

"Well," said David, "Nancy's got to be 'sponsible, because I took care of her mouse."

"If I were you," said Ambrose with a superior air, "I wouldn't use such long words; you never say them right."

"I say," interrupted Pennie, putting down her book, "what do you all like best when you go to Nearminster? I know what *I* like best."

"Well, what is it?" said Ambrose; "you say first, and then Nancy, and then me, and then David."

"Well," said Pennie, clasping her knees with much enjoyment, "what I like best is going to church in the Cathedral in the afternoon. When it's a little bit dusky, you know, but not lighted up, and all the pillars look misty, and a long way off, and there are very few people. And then the boys sing, and you feel quite good and just a little bit sad; I can't think why it is that I never feel like that in our church; I suppose it's a cathedral feeling. That's what I like best. Now you, Nancy."

"Why," said Nancy without the least hesitation. "I like that little Chinese mandarin that stands on the mantel-piece in Miss Unity's sitting-room, and wags its head."

"And *I* like the drive back here best," said Ambrose, "because, when we're going there's only Miss Unity to see at the end; but when we get here there are all the animals and things."

"I don't call that liking Nearminster. I call it liking home," said Nancy. "Now, it's your turn, David."

"I don't know what I like best," said David solemnly. "I only know what I like least."

"What's that?"

"Miss Unity," said David with decision.

"Should you call her very ugly?" inquired Ambrose.

"Yes, of course, quite hideous," replied Nancy indistinctly, with her paint-brush in her mouth.

"Well, I'm not quite sure," said Pennie; "once I saw her eyes look quite nice, as if they had a light shining at the back of them."

"Like that face Andrew made for us out of a hollow pumpkin, with a candle inside?" suggested Nancy.

"You're always so stupid, Nancy!" said Ambrose scornfully. "I know what Pennie means about Miss Unity; *I've* seen her eyes look nice too. Don't you remember, too, how kind she was when Dickie was so rude to her? I've never been so afraid of her since that."

The next day the party started for Nearminster in the

wagonette, David sitting in front with his feet resting comfortably on his own little trunk. Andrew, who drove, allowed him to hold the whip sometimes, and the end of the reins—so it was quite easy to fancy himself a coachman; but this delightful position did not make him forget other things. Beckoning to Nancy, who stood with the rest on the rectory steps, he lifted a solemn finger.

"Remember!" he said.

Nancy nodded, the wagonette drove away followed by wavings, and good-byes, and shrieking messages from the children, and was soon out of sight.

"That was like Charles the First," said Pennie; "don't you remember just before they cut off his head—"

"Oh, don't!" said Nancy; "pray, don't talk about Charles the First out of lesson time."

Chapter Five.

Miss Unity.

It was a lonely life which Miss Unity Cheffins lived at Nearminster, but she had become so used to it that it did not occur to her to wish for any other. Far far in the distance she could remember a time when everything had not been so quiet and still round her—when she was one of a group of children who had made the old house in the Close echo with their little hurrying footsteps and laughing voices. One by one those voices had become silent and the footsteps had hastened away, and Miss Unity was left alone to fill the empty rooms as she best might with the memories of the past. That was long long ago, and now her days were all just alike, as formal and even as the trimly-kept Close outside her door. And she liked them to be so; any variety or change would have been irksome to her. She liked to know that exactly as eight o'clock sounded from the cathedral Bridget would bring her a cup of tea, would pull up her blind to a certain height, and would remark, "A fine morning, ma'am," or "A dull morning," as the case might be. At eleven o'clock, wet or dry, she would sally forth into the town to do the light part of her marketing and cast a thoughtful eye on the price of vegetables; after which, girt with a large linen apron, and her head protected by a mob-cap, she would proceed to dust and wash her cherished china. From much loneliness she had formed a habit of talking quietly to herself during these operations; but no one could have understood her, for she only uttered the fag-ends of her thoughts aloud.

The Chinese mandarin which Nancy admired was the object of Miss Unity's fondest care; some bygone association was doubtless connected with him, for she seldom failed to utter some husky little sentences of endearment while she lingered over his grotesque person with tender touches of her feather brush. So the day went on. After her dinner, if the weather were fair, she would perhaps deck herself with a black silk mantilla and a tall bonnet with nodding flowers, and go out to visit some old friend. A muffin, a cup of tea, and perhaps a little cathedral gossip would follow; and then Miss Unity, stepping primly across the Close, reached the dull shelter of her own home again, and was alone for the rest of the evening. At ten o'clock she read prayers to Bridget and the little maid, and so to bed.

The even course of these days was only disturbed twice in the year—once by Mr and Mrs Hawthorn's visit to Nearminster, and once by Miss Unity's visit to Easney. These were important events to her, anticipated for months, not exactly with pleasure; for, though she was really fond of her friends, she was shy, and to be put out of her usual habits was, besides, a positive torture to her. Then there were the children! Troublesome little riddles Miss Unity often found them, impossible to understand; and it is a question whether she or they were the more uncomfortable when they were together. For she had an idea, gathered from some dim recollection of the past, that children needed constant correction and reproof; and she felt sure Mary Hawthorn neglected her duty in this respect and was over-indulgent. So, being a most conscientious woman, she tried to supply this shortcoming, and the result was not a happy one.

She was ill at ease with all the children, but of Dickie she was fairly frightened, for Dickie had disgraced herself at her very first introduction. Seeing Miss Unity's grim face framed by the nodding bonnet bending down to kiss her, the child looked up and said with a sweet smile, "Ugly lady!"

There was no disguising it, for Dickie's utterance had the clearness of a bell, and a horrified silence fell on the assembly.

"Don't be naughty, Dickie," said Mrs Hawthorn reprovingly; "say, 'How do you do?' directly."

But Miss Unity had straightened herself up and turned away with an odd look in her eyes.

"Don't scold the child, Mary," she said; "she's not naughty, she's only honest."

From that time Pennie never considered Miss Unity quite ugly, and indeed her features were not so much ugly as rugged and immovable. When her feelings were stirred she was not ugly at all; for they were good, kind feelings, and made her whole face look pleasant. So little happened in her life, however, that they generally remained shut up as in a sort of prison and were seldom called forth; people, therefore, who did not know her often thought her cross. But Miss Unity was not cross—she was only lonely and dull because she had so little to love. Nothing could have passed off better than the Hawthorns' visit on this particular occasion, and indeed when David was with her Mrs Hawthorn never feared the unlucky accidents which were apt to occur with the other children. He was so deliberate and careful by nature that there was no risk of his knocking down the china, or treading on the cat's tail, or on the train of Miss Unity's gown. Nancy did all these things frequently, however hard she tried to be good, and was besides very restive under reproof and ready to answer pertly.

On the whole Miss Unity liked to have the grave little David with her better than the other children, though she sometimes felt when she found his solemn and disapproving gaze fixed upon her. David on his side had his opinions, though he said little, and he had long ago made up his mind that he did not like Miss Unity at all. So he was sorry to find, when the day came for leaving Nearminster, that she was going back to Easney with them instead of making her visit later in the year. It would not be nearly as pleasant as driving alone with his father and mother, he thought; for now he could not ask questions on the way, unless he talked to Andrew, and he was always so silent.

When the wagonette came round there were so many little packages belonging to Miss Unity that it was quite difficult to stow them away, and as fast as that was done Bridget brought out more. Not that there was much luggage altogether, but it consisted in such a number of oddly-shaped parcels and small boxes that it was both puzzling and distracting to know where to put them. Mr Hawthorn was busy for a good quarter of an hour disposing of Miss Unity's property; while David looked on, keenly interested, and full of faith in his father's capacity.

"That's all, I think," said Mr Hawthorn triumphantly at last, as he emerged from the depths of the wagonette, and surveyed his labours; "there's not much room left for us, certainly, but I daresay we shall manage."

As he spoke Bridget came out of the house carrying a waterproof bundle, bristling with umbrellas and parasols.

"Oh, dear me!" exclaimed the vicar in a discouraged voice, "is that to go? Does your mistress want all those umbrellas?"

"She wouldn't like to go without 'em, sir," replied Bridget.

"Where *shall* you put them, father?" asked David in quite an excited manner.

That was indeed a question, but it was at length solved by Mr Hawthorn deciding to walk, and the wagonette was ready to proceed, David sitting in front as usual. After several efforts to make Andrew talk he fell back for amusement on his own thoughts, and in recognising all the well-known objects they passed on the road. Presently they came to a certain little grey cottage, and then he knew they were halfway home. It had honeysuckle growing over the porch, and a row of bee-hives in the garden, which was generally bright and gay with flowers; just now, however, it all looked withered and unattractive, except that on one tree there still hung some very red apples, though it was the beginning of November. That reminded David of Antony, who had a great weakness for apples. He smiled to himself, and felt glad that he should see his pet so soon.

After this cottage there was a long steep hill to go up, and here Ruby the horse always waited for Andrew to get down and walk. David might really drive now, and even flick at Ruby's fat sides with the whip, which was pleasant, but did not make the least difference to his speed.

When they had reached the top of the hill, the little square tower of Easney church could just be seen, and the chimneys of the vicarage, but though they looked near, there were still nearly four miles to drive. Now it was all downhill, and Ruby pounded along at an even trot, which seemed to make a sort of accompaniment to David's thoughts—

To market, to market,
To buy a fat pig;
Home again, home again,
Jig a jig, jig!

it said, over and over again. "I wonder whether Antony will know me!" thought David.

Five minutes more and the carriage stopped at the white gate, and Andrew getting down to open it, David drove in a masterly manner up to the front door, where Ambrose, Pennie, and Dickie were assembled to welcome the return. Amidst the bustle which followed, while Miss Unity's belongings were being unpacked and carried indoors under the watchful eye of their owner, David slipped down from his perch and hurried away towards the kitchen-garden; Antony lived there, and he would go and see him first of all. As he ran along the narrow path, bordered with fruit-trees, he stooped to pick up a wrinkled red apple which had fallen. "He's *so* fond of 'em!" thought he, as he put it in his pocket. There was the sty, and now he should soon hear the low grunt so delightful to his ears. All was silent, however, and he went on more slowly, with a slight feeling of dread, for somehow the sty had a strangely empty look about it. "He's eating," said David encouragingly to himself; but even as he said so he stood still, quite afraid to go any nearer. Then he called gently: "Choug, choug, choug." No sign of life. No inquiring black snout peering over the edge. Unable to bear the uncertainty, he rushed forward and looked into the sty.

Empty! Yes, quite empty—Antony's straw bed was there, and the remains of some food in his trough, but no Antony!

David stood staring at the desolate dwelling for some minutes, hardly able to believe his eyes; then with a thrill of hope he said to himself:

"He must have got out. He must be somewhere in the garden;" and he turned round to go and search for him. As he did so, he saw a small dejected figure coming down the path towards him with downcast face and lagging step. It was Nancy —grief in every feature, and guilt in every movement. One glance was enough for David; he understood it all now, and he flushed angrily, and turned his back upon her, clenching his fists tightly. She came slowly up and stood close to him; she was crying.

"Oh, Davie," she said. "I am so sorry."

"Where's Antony?" said David in a muffled voice without

looking at her.

"He's gone."

"Where?"

"Back to the farm."

"Why?"

"Andrew took him. He found him eating the spinach, and he said he must obey orders. And I asked Miss Grey to stop him, and she said she couldn't interfere —"

Nancy stopped and gasped.

"Then," said David sternly, "you didn't fasten his gate."

"Oh, I *thought* I did," said Nancy, beginning to sob again in an agonised manner; "but I forgot to put that stick through the staple, and he must have pushed it open. I am so sorry."

"That's no good at all," said David with a trembling lip; "Antony's gone."

"I'll give you anything of mine to make up," said Nancy eagerly — "my bantam hen, or my dormouse, or my white kitten."

"I don't want anything of yours," said David, "I want my own pig."

Nancy was silent, except for some little convulsive sobs. Presently she made a last effort.

"Please, Davie," she said humbly, "won't you forgive me? I *am* so sorry."

David turned round. His face was very red, but he spoke slowly and quietly:

"No," he said, "I won't forgive you. I never mean to. You promised to take care of Antony, and you haven't. You're *very* wicked."

Then he went away and left Nancy in floods of tears by the empty sty.

Everyone sympathised with David at first, and was sorry for his loss, though perhaps no one quite understood what a great one it was to him; but there was another feeling mingled with his grief for Antony, which was even stronger, and that was anger towards his sister. David had a deep sense of justice, and it seemed hard to him that he alone should suffer for Nancy's wrong-doing. When he saw her after a time as merry and gay as though Antony had never existed, he felt as hard as stone, and would neither speak to her nor join in any game in which she took part. She ought to be punished, he thought, and made to feel as unhappy as he did. Poor little Davie! he was very miserable in those days, and sadly changed, for his once loving heart was torn with grief and anger, which are both hard to bear, but anger far the worse of the two. So he moped about mournfully alone, and no one took much notice of him, for people got tired of trying to comfort him and persuade him to forgive. Even his mother was unsuccessful:

"You ought to forgive and forget, Davie," said she.

"I *can't* forget Antony," replied David, "and I don't want to forgive Nancy. I'd rather *not*."

"But she would be the first to forget any wrong thing you did to her," continued Mrs Hawthorn.

"Nancy *always* forgets," said David, "wrong things and right things too."

Mrs Hawthorn was silenced, for this was strictly true.

"I don't know what to make of David," she said to her husband afterwards. "I would ask you to let him have the pig back, but I don't think he ought to have it while he shows this unforgiving spirit."

"Let him alone," said the vicar. "Leave it to time."

So David was left alone; but time went on and did not

seem to soften his feelings in the least, and this was at last brought about by a very unexpected person.

One morning Miss Unity, who had now been staying some time at Easney, went out to take a little air in the garden: it was rather damp under foot, for it had rained in the night, but now the sun shone brightly, and she stepped forth, well protected by over-shoes and thick shawl, with the intention of taking exercise for exactly a quarter of an hour.

From the direction of the Wilderness she heard shouts and laughter which warned her of the children's whereabouts, and she turned at once into another path which led to the kitchen-garden.

"How Mary does let those children run wild!" she said to herself, "and Pennie getting a great girl, too. As for Miss Grey, she's a perfect cipher, and doesn't look after them a bit. If they were *my* children—"

But here Miss Unity's reflections were checked. Lifting her eyes she saw at the end of the narrow path a low shed which looked like a pig-sty; by it was a plank, raised at each end on a stone, so as to form a rough bench, and on this there crouched a small disconsolate figure. It was bent nearly double, and had its face buried in its hands, so that only a rough shock of very light hair was visible; but though she could not see any features Miss Unity knew at once that it was David mourning for his pig.

Her first impulse was to turn round and go quickly away, for she had gathered from what she had heard of the affair that he was a very naughty, sulky little boy; as she looked, however, she saw by a slight heaving movement of the shoulder that he was crying quietly, and her heart was stirred with sudden pity:

"It's a real grief to the child, that's evident, though it's only about a pig," she said to herself, and, yielding to another impulse, she walked on towards him instead of going back. But after all it was a difficult situation when she got close to him, for she did not know what to say, although she felt an increasing desire to give him comfort. At any rate it was useless to stand there in silence looking at that little bowed head; would it be better to sit down by him, perhaps? she wondered, casting a doubtful eye on the decidedly dirty plank. Miss Unity was delicately particular, and her whole soul recoiled from dirt and dust, so it was really with heroic resolution that she suddenly folded her nice grey gown closely about her and took a seat, stiffly erect, by David's side. When there she felt impelled to pat his head gently with two long fingers, and say softly: "Poor little boy!"

David had watched all Miss Unity's movements narrowly through a chink in his fingers, though he kept his face closely hidden, and when she sat down beside him he was so surprised that he stopped crying. He wondered what she was going to say. She would scold him, of course, everyone scolded him now, and he set his teeth sullenly and prepared to defend himself. Then the unexpected kind words fell on his ear, and he could not help bursting into fresh tears, and sobbed as if his heart would break. It was partly for Antony, partly for Nancy, partly for himself that he was crying; he was so tired of being naughty, and he wanted so much to be made good again.

Miss Unity was sadly perplexed by the result of her efforts; she seemed to have made matters worse instead of better, and she sat for some minutes in silent dismay by the side of the sobbing David. But having begun she felt she must go on, and taking advantage of a little lull she presently said:

"Was it a nice pig, David?"

"B–b–beautiful."

"And you miss it?"

This was so evident a fact that David seemed to think it needed no answer, and Miss Unity continued:

"It's sad to lose anything we know and love. Very hard to bear. It's quite natural and right to be sorry."

David took his hands away from his face, which was curiously marked by dirty fingers and tears, and lifted a pair of blurred blue eyes to Miss Unity. He was listening, and she felt encouraged to proceed:

"But though it's hard, there is something else that is much worse; do you know what that is?"

"No," said David.

"To be angry with anyone we love," said Miss Unity solemnly; "that is a very bitter feeling, and hurts us very much. All the while we have it in our hearts we can't be happy, because anger and love are fighting together."

David's eyes grew rounder and larger. Could this really be Miss Unity? He was deeply impressed.

"And they fight," she went on, "until one is killed. Very often love is stronger, but sometimes it is anger that conquers, and then sad things follow. In this way, David, much evil has happened in the world from time to time."

Miss Unity paused. She felt that she was getting on very well, and was surprised at her own success, for David had stopped crying, and was staring at her with absorbed interest. She went on:

"When once we let anger drive love quite out of our hearts all manner of bad things enter; but we don't often succeed in doing it, because love is so great and strong. Do you know why you're so unhappy just now?"

"Because I've lost Antony," said David at once.

"Yes, that is one reason, but there is a bigger one. It is because you are angry with Nancy."

David hung his head.

"You're fond of Nancy, Davie? I've heard your mother say that you and she are favourite playfellows."

"No," said David, "not now. She promised to shut Antony's gate—and she forgot."

Miss Unity stopped a moment to think; then she said:

"Would you be happier, David, if Nancy were to be punished?"

"Yes."

"Why?"

"Because it would be fair."

"Well—you know it's Nancy's birthday soon, and she has to choose what present I shall give her?"

David nodded his head. He knew it very well; and not only that, he knew what Nancy was going to choose, for she had confided to him as a great secret that her heart was set on a kitchen-range for the doll's house.

"When she chooses, would you like me to say: 'No, Nancy. Because you were careless and forgot David's pig I shall give you nothing this year?'"

Miss Unity waited eagerly for the answer. How she hoped it would be "No." She had not been so anxious for anything for a long time.

But David raised his head, gazed at her calmly, and said quite distinctly:

"Yes."

Miss Unity sighed as she got up from her lowly seat.

"Very well, David," she said, "it shall be so; but I am sorry you will not forgive your sister."

She went sadly back to the house, thinking to herself:

"Of course *I* could not persuade where others have failed. It was foolish to try. I have no influence with children. I ought to have remembered that."

But she was mistaken. That night when she was dressing for dinner there was a little knock at her door, very low down as though from somebody of short stature. She opened it, and there was David.

"If you please," he said, "I've come to say that I'd rather you gave Nancy the kitchen-range—I mean, whatever she chooses for her birthday."

"Then you've forgiven her?" asked Miss Unity excitedly.

"Yes," said David. "Good-night, because it's bed-time. Nurse said I was to go back directly."

He held out his hand, and also raised a pursed-up mouth towards Miss Unity, which meant that he wished to be kissed.

Feeling the honour deeply she stooped and kissed him, and her eyes followed the little square figure wistfully as it trotted down the passage to the nursery; when it disappeared she turned into her room again with a warmer feeling about her heart than she had known for many a day.

Three days after this was Nancy's birthday, and although the kitchen-range did not appear she hopped and skipped and looked so brimful of delight that David could not help asking: "What are you so pleased about?"

"Come with me," was Nancy's reply, "and I'll show you Miss Unity's birthday present. It's the best of all."

She hurried David into the garden, and up to the pig-sty —empty no longer! There was Antony as lively as ever, and ready to greet his master with a cheerful grunt!

"There," she said, in the intervals of a dance of triumph,

"I and Andrew fetched him home. Father said we might. I asked Miss Unity to ask him to have him back for a birthday present. And she did. She was so kind; and I don't think she's ugly now at all."

Nor did David; and he never said again that the thing he liked least at Nearminster was Miss Unity, for he had a long memory for benefits as well as for injuries.

Chapter Six.

Ethelwyn.

"Oh, dear me!" said Pennie, looking at herself in the glass over the nursery mantel-shelf; "it *is* ugly, and *so* uncomfortable. I wish I needn't wear it."

"It," was Pennie's new winter bonnet, and certainly it was not very becoming; it was made of black plush with a very deep brim, out of which her little pointed face peered mournfully, and seemed almost swallowed up. There was one exactly like it for Nancy, and the bonnets had just come from Miss Griggs, the milliner at Nearminster, where they had been ordered a week ago. "Do you come and try yours on, Miss Pennie," said Nurse as she unpacked them, "there's no getting hold of Miss Nancy."

So Pennie put it on with a little secret hope that it might be a prettier bonnet than the last; she looked in the glass, and then followed the exclamation with which this chapter begins.

"I don't see anything amiss with it," said Nurse, who stood with her head on one side, and the other bonnet perched on her hand. "They're as alike as two pins," she added, twirling it round admiringly.

"They're both just as ugly as they can be," said Pennie mournfully; "but mine's sure to look worse than Nancy's—it always does. And they never *will* stay on," she added in a still more dejected voice, "unless I keep on catching at the strings in front with my chin."

"Oh, well, Miss Pennie," said Nurse, "your head will grow to it, and you ought to be thankful to have such a nice warm bonnet. How would you like to go about with just a shawl over your head, like them gypsies we saw the other day?"

"*Very much indeed,*" said Pennie, who had now taken off the bonnet and was looking at it ruefully. "There was one gypsy who had a red handkerchief, which looked much prettier than this ugly old thing."

"You oughtn't to mind how things look," returned Nurse. "You think too much of outsides, Miss Pennie."

"But the outside of a bonnet is the only part that matters," replied Pennie.

She was quite prepared to continue the subject, but this was not the case with Nurse.

"I've no time for argufying, miss," she said as she put the bonnets carefully back into their boxes. "I'm sure my mistress will like them very much. They're just as she ordered them." And so the subject was dismissed, and Pennie felt that she was again a victim.

For, as Nurse had said, Pennie *did* care a great deal about outsides, and she thought it hard sometimes that she and Nancy must always be dressed alike, for the same things did not suit them at all. Probably this very bonnet which was such a trial to Pennie would be a suitable frame for Nancy's round rosy face, and look quite nice. It was certainly hard. Pennie loved all beautiful things, from the flowers in the garden and fields to the yellow curls on Cicely's ruffled head, and it often troubled her to feel that with pretty things all round her she did not look pretty herself. So the winter bonnet cast quite a gloom on her for the moment, and although it may seem a small trial to sensible people it was a large one to Pennie. How often she had sighed over the straight little serge frocks which she and Nancy always wore, and secretly longed for brighter colours and more flowing lines, and now this ugly dark bonnet had come to make things worse. It would make her feel like a blot in a fair white copybook, to walk about in it when the beautiful clean snow covered the earth. What a pity that everything in the world was not pretty!

Pennie's whole soul went out towards beauty, and anyone with a pretty face might be sure of her loving worship and admiration. "All is not gold that glitters, Miss Pennie," Nurse would say, or, "Handsome is that handsome does;" but it made no impression at all; Pennie continued to feel sure that what looked pretty *must* be good, and that a fair outside meant perfection within.

She stood thoughtfully watching Nurse as she put the bonnets away. It *would* be nice to wear a scarlet handkerchief over your head like that gypsy. Such a lovely colour! And then there would be no tormenting "caught back" feeling when the wind blew, which made it necessary to press the chin firmly on the strings to keep that miserable bonnet on at all. And besides these advantages it would be much cheaper, for she had heard her mother say that Miss Griggs' things were *so* expensive; "but then," Mrs Hawthorn had added, "the best of them is that they *do* last." Pennie thought that decidedly "the worst" of them, for she and Nancy would have to wear those bonnets for at least two winters before they showed any signs of wearing out—indeed, they had been made rather large in the head on purpose.

But it was of no use to think about it any more now, so with a little sigh she turned away and went back to her dolls, prepared to treat the ugly one, Jemima, with even more than usual severity. Jemima was the oldest doll of the lot, made of a sort of papier-maché; her hair was painted black and arranged in short fat curls; her face, from frequent washing and punishment, had become of a leaden hue, and was full of dents and bruises; her nose was quite flat, and she had lost one arm; in her best days she had been plain, but she was now hideous. And no wonder! Poor Jemima had been through enough trials to mar the finest beauty. She had been the victim at so many scenes of torture and executions that there was scarcely a noted sufferer in the whole of the History of England whom she had not, at some time or other, represented. To be burnt alive was quite a common thing to Jemima, and sometimes, descending from the position of martyr to that of criminal, she was hanged as a murderer! In an unusually bloodthirsty moment Ambrose had once suggested *really* putting out her eyes with red-hot gauffering-irons, but this was overruled, and Jemima's eyes, pale blue and quite expressionless, continued to stare placidly on the stake, gibbet, or block, as the case might be.

It was a relief to Pennie just now to cuff and scold Jemima, and to pet the Lady Dulcibella, who was a wax doll with a lovely pink and white complexion, and real golden hair and eyelashes. She had everything befitting a doll of her station and appearance—a comfortable bed with white curtains, an arm-chair with a chintz cushion, private brushes and combs, and an elegant travelling trunk. Her life altogether was a contrast to Jemima's, who never went to bed at all, and had no possessions except one ragged old red dress; nevertheless, it is possible that Dulcibella with all her elegance would have been the more easily spared of the two.

Nancy soon joined Pennie, and the little girls became so absorbed in their play that they were still busy when tea-time came; they hurried down-stairs to the schoolroom, for Miss Grey was particular about punctuality, and found that David and Ambrose were already seated, each with his own special mug at his side; mother was in the room too, talking to Miss Grey about an open letter which she held in her hand.

Mrs Hawthorn always paid the children a visit at schoolroom tea, and they generally had something wonderful to tell her saved up for this occasion—things which had occurred during their walk, or perhaps exciting details about the various pet animals. Sometimes she in her turn had news for them, and when Pennie saw the open letter she changed her intention of saying that the bonnets had come home, and waited quietly. Perhaps mother had something interesting to tell.

Pennie was right, for Mrs Hawthorn presently made an announcement of such a startling character that the new bonnets sank at once into insignificance.

"Children," she said, "a little girl is coming to stay with you."

Now such a thing had never happened before, and it was so astonishing that they all stared at their mother in silence with half-uplifted mugs, and slices of bread and butter in their hands. Then all at once they began to pour forth a torrent of questions: — What is she like? Where does she live? How old is she? What is her name?

Mrs Hawthorn held up her hand.

"One at a time," she said. "If you will be quiet you shall hear all about it. This little girl lives in London. Her mother is a very old friend of mine, though you have never seen her, and I have asked her to let her little daughter come here for a visit. She is about Pennie's age, and her name is Ethelwyn."

"What a long one!" said Nancy; "must we call her all of it?"

"I think it's a beautiful name," said Pennie. "Almost as good as 'Dulcibella.' And then we might call her 'Ethel,' or 'Winnie,' they're both pretty."

"Well, you can settle that afterwards," said their mother. "You must wait and see what she likes best to be called. And that reminds me to say that I hope my children will be hospitable to their guest. Do you know what that means?"

"I know," said Ambrose, gulping a piece of bread and butter very quickly in his haste to be first. "Let *me* say. It means taking care of people when they're ill."

"Not quite right," said Mrs Hawthorn. "You are thinking of 'hospital,' which is a different thing, though both words come from the same idea; can you tell, Pennie?"

"It means being kind, doesn't it?" said Pennie.

"It means something more than that. What do you say, Davie?"

"Always to give her the biggest piece," said David, with his eyes thoughtfully fixed on the pile of bread and butter.

Nancy was then appealed to, but she always refused to apply her mind out of lesson hours, and only shook her head.

"Well," said Mrs Hawthorn, "I think Davie's explanation is about the best, for hospitality does mean giving our friends the best we have. But it means something more, for you might give Ethelwyn the biggest piece of everything, and yet she might not enjoy her visit at all. But if you try to make her happy in the way *she likes best*, and consider her amusement and comfort before your own, you will be hospitable, and I shall be very pleased with you all. I expect, however, she will be chiefly Pennie and Nancy's companion, because, as she has no brothers and sisters, she may not care about the games you all play together. She has not been used to boys, and might find them a little rough and noisy."

Pennie drew herself up a little. It would be rather nice to have a friend of her very own, and already she saw herself Ethelwyn's sole support and adviser.

The children continued to ask questions until there was nothing else to be learnt about Ethelwyn, and she was made the subject of conversation after their mother left the room, and until tea was over. They made various plans for the amusement of the expected guest.

"I can show her my pig," said David.

"And the rabbits and the jackdaw and the owl," added Ambrose.

"Oh, I don't suppose she'll care at all about such common things as pigs and rabbits," said Pennie rather scornfully, for the very name of Ethelwyn had a sort of superior sound.

"Then she'll be a stupid," said Ambrose.

"Owdacious," added David.

"Davie," said Miss Grey, "where did you hear that word?"

"Andrew says it," answered David triumphantly; "he says Antony grows owdacious."

A lively argument followed, for David could not be brought to understand for some time why Andrew's expressions were not equally fit for little boys and gardeners. Ethelwyn was for the time forgotten by everyone except Pennie, who continued to think about her all that evening. Indeed, for days afterwards her mind was full of nothing else; she wondered what she was like, and how she would talk, and she had Ethelwyn so much on the brain that she could not keep her out of her head even in lesson time. She came floating across the pages of the History of England while Pennie was reading aloud, and caused her to make strange mistakes in the names of the Saxon kings.

"Ethelbert, not Ethelwyn, Pennie," Miss Grey would say for the twentieth time, and then with a little impatient shake Pennie would wake up from her day-dreams, and try to fix her mind on the matter in hand. But it was really difficult, for those kings seemed to follow each other so fast, and to do so much the same things, and even to have names so much alike, that it was almost impossible to have clear ideas about them. Pennie's attention soon wandered away again to a more attractive subject: Ethelwyn! it was certainly a nice name to have, and seemed to mean all sorts of interesting things; how small and poor the name of Pennie sounded after it! shortened to Pen, as it was sometimes, it was worse still. No doubt Ethelwyn would be pretty. She would have long yellow hair, Pennie decided, not plaited up in a pig-tail like her own and Nancy's, but falling over her shoulders in a nice fluffy way like the Lady Dulcibella's. Pennie often felt sorry that there was no fluffiness at all about her hair, or that of her brothers and sisters; their heads all looked so neat and tight, and indeed they could not do otherwise under Nurse's vigorous treatment, for she went on the principle that anything rough was untidy. Even Dickie's hair, which wanted to curl, was sternly checked, and kept closely cropped like a boy's; it was only Cicely's that was allowed at present to do as it liked and wave about in soft little rings of gold.

Pennie made her plans and thought her thoughts, and often went to bed with Ethelwyn's imaginary figure so strongly before her that she had wonderful dreams. Ethelwyn took the shape of the "Fair One with the Golden Locks," in the fairy book, and stood before her with yellow hair quite down to her feet—beautiful, gracious, smiling. Even in the daylight Pennie could not quite get rid of the idea, and so, long before she had seen her, the name of Ethelwyn came to mean, in her romantic little mind, everything that was lovely and desirable.

And at last Ethelwyn came. It was an exciting moment, for the children were so unused to strangers that they were prepared to look upon their visitor with deep curiosity. They were nevertheless shy, and it had occurred to David and Nancy that the cupboard under the stairs would be a favourable position from which to take cautious observations when she arrived.

Ambrose, therefore, and Pennie were the only two ready to receive their guest, for Dickie was busy with her own affairs in the nursery; they waited in the schoolroom with nervous impatience, and presently the drawing-room bell rang twice, which was always a signal that the children were wanted.

"That's for us," said Pennie. "Come, Ambrose."

But Ambrose held back. "*You* go," he said. "Mother doesn't want me."

And Pennie, after trying a few persuasions, was obliged to go alone. But when she got to the door and heard voices inside the room she found it difficult to go in, and stood on the mat for some minutes before she could make up her mind to turn the handle. She looked down at her pinafore and saw that it was a good deal crumpled, and an unlucky ink-spot stared at her like a little black eye in the very middle of it; surely, too, Nurse had drawn back her hair more tightly than usual from her face. Altogether she felt unequal to meeting the unknown but elegant Ethelwyn.

It must be done, however, and at last she turned the handle quickly and went into the room. Mrs Hawthorn was sitting by the fire, and in front of her stood a little girl. Her hair *was* fluffy and yellow, just as Pennie had thought, and hung down her back in nice waves escaping from the prettiest possible quilted bonnet (how different from that black plush one upstairs!) This was dark blue like her dress, and she carried a dear little quilted muff to match. Her features were neat and straight, and her large violet eyes had long lashes curling upwards; there was really quite a striking likeness between her face and the Lady Dulcibella's, except that the cheeks of the latter were bright pink, and Ethelwyn was delicately pale.

Pennie noticed all this as she advanced slowly up the room, deeply conscious of the crumpled pinafore and the ink-spot.

"This is Pennie," said her mother, and Ethelwyn immediately held out her hand, and said, "How do you do?" in rather a prim voice and without any shyness at all.

"Now I shall give Ethelwyn into your care, Pennie," continued Mrs Hawthorn. "You may take her into the garden and show her the pets, or if she likes it better you may go upstairs and play with your dolls. Make her as happy as you can, and I shall see you all again at tea-time."

The two little girls left the room together, and Pennie led the way silently to the garden, giving furtive glances now and then at her visitor. She felt sure that Ethelwyn would be surprised and pleased, because mother had said that in London people seldom had gardens; but her companion made no remark at all, and Pennie put the question which had been a good deal on her mind:

"What do you like to be called?"

"My name's Ethelwyn," said the little girl.

"Yes, I know," said Pennie. "Mother told us. But I mean, what are you called for short?"

"I'm *always* called Ethelwyn. Father and mother don't approve of names being shortened."

"Oh!" said Pennie deeply impressed. Then feeling it necessary to assert herself, she added: "*My* name's Penelope Mary Hawthorn; but I'm always called Pennie, and sometimes the children call me Pen."

Ethelwyn made no answer; she was attentively observing

Pennie's blue serge frock, and presently asked:

"What's your best dress?"

"It's the same as this," said Pennie, looking down at it meekly, "only newer."

"Mine's velveteen," said Ethelwyn, "the new shade, you know—a sort of mouse colour. Nurse says I look like a picture in it. Do you always wear pinafores?"

Before Pennie had time to answer they had arrived at the Wilderness, and were now joined by Nancy and the two boys, who came shyly forward to shake hands.

"These are our gardens," said Pennie, doing the honours of the Wilderness; "that's mine, and that's Dickie's, and the well belongs to the others. They dug it themselves."

Ethelwyn looked round, with her little pointed nose held rather high in the air:

"Why don't you keep it neater?" she said. "What an untidy place!"

It was a blow to Pennie to hear this, but the truth of it struck her forcibly, and she now saw for the first time that to a stranger the Wilderness might not be very attractive. There were, of course, no flowers now, and Dickie had tumbled a barrowful of leaves on to the middle of Pennie's border, which was further adorned by a heap of oyster shells, with which David intended some day to build a grotto. It looked more like a rubbish heap than a garden, and the close neighbourhood of the well did not improve it. There was only one cheerful object in the Wilderness just now, and that was a little monthly rose-bush in Dickie's plot of ground, which, in spite of most unfavourable circumstances, bore two bright pink blossoms.

After glancing scornfully round, Ethelwyn stooped and stretched out her hand to pick the roses; but Pennie caught hold of her dress in alarm.

"Oh, you mustn't," she cried; "they're Dickie's."

Ethelwyn looked up astonished.

"Who's Dickie?" she said; "what does he want them for?"

"It isn't 'he,' it's 'she,'" said Nancy; "she's the youngest but one, and she's saving them for mother's birthday."

"Wouldn't it be a joke," said Ethelwyn laughing, "to pick them? She'd never know where they'd gone."

Pennie could not see anything funny in this idea at all, but she remembered what Mrs Hawthorn had said about making their guest happy in her own way, and she felt obliged to answer:

"If you want to do it *very* much you may."

She was sorry to see that Ethelwyn immediately pulled both the little roses off the tree, but tried to excuse her in her own mind. She did not understand, perhaps, how much Dickie wanted them. Such a pretty graceful creature as Ethelwyn *could* not do anything purposely unkind.

Nancy, however, not the least dazzled by Ethelwyn's appearance, was boiling with anger.

"I call that—" she began; but Pennie nudged her violently and whispered: "She's a visitor," and the outspoken opinion was checked.

David, too, turned the general attention another way just then; he came gravely up to Ethelwyn and inquired:

"Do you like animals?"

"Animals?" said Ethelwyn; "oh, you mean pets. Yes, I like them sometimes."

"Then I'll show you my pig," said David.

"A pig!" exclaimed Ethelwyn in rather a squeaky voice of surprise; "what a nasty, dirty thing to have for a pet! Don't you mean *pug*?"

"No, I don't," said David; "I mean pig."

"But it's not a common sort of pig at all," put in Pennie hastily, for she saw her brother's face getting crimson with anger, "and it's beautifully clean and clever. It shakes hands."

"We've got lots of animals," added Ambrose, "only you must come round to the barn to see them."

"Well," said Ethelwyn as the children all moved away, David rather sulkily, with hands in his pockets, "I *never* heard of a pig as a pet. I don't believe it's a proper sort of pet at all. Now, *I've* got a little tiny toy terrier at home, and he has a collar with silver bells. I *had* a canary, but Nurse left its cage on the window-ledge in a high wind, and it blew right down on the pavement from the very tip-top of the house, so it died."

"Oh," cried Nancy, horror-stricken, "how dreadful! Weren't you sorry?"

"Not very," said Ethelwyn coolly. "You see I'd had it a long time, and I was rather tired of it, and I often forgot to feed it."

The animals were now visited, and introduced by their respective owners, but without exciting much interest in Ethelwyn, for whatever she saw it always appeared that she had something far better at home. Even Antony's lively talents failed to move her, and, though she *could* not say she had a nicer pig herself, she observed calmly:

"Ah, you should see the animals in the Zoological Gardens!"

And to this there was no reply.

Then she was taken to swing in the barn, and this proved a more successful entertainment, for as long as the children would swing her Ethelwyn was content to be swung. When, however, Nancy boldly remarked:

"It's someone else's turn now," she was not quite so pleased, and soon said in a discontented voice:

"I'm tired of this. Let's go indoors and see your playthings."

Here it was the same thing over again, for she found something slighting to say even of the Lady Dulcibella, who was sitting prepared to receive visitors in her best pink frock.

"Can she talk?" asked Ethelwyn. "*My* last new doll says 'papa,' 'mama.'"

Then her eye fell on the luckless Jemima, who, in her usual mean attire, was sitting in the background with her head drooping helplessly, for it had been loosened by constant execution.

"Oh," cried Ethelwyn, pouncing upon her with more animation than she had yet shown, "here's a fright!"

She held the doll up by its frock, so that its legs and one remaining arm dangled miserably in the air.

"It's only Jemima," said Pennie. She was vexed that Ethelwyn had seen her at all, and there was something painful in having her held up to the general scorn.

Ethelwyn began to giggle.

"Why do you keep a guy like that?" she said. "Why don't you burn it?"

"Well, so we do," replied Nancy, "very often. We burnt her only last week."

"She was Joan of Arc," explained Pennie. "Only make-believe, you know. Not real flames."

Ethelwyn stared. "What odd games you play!" she said. "I never heard of them. But I know one thing: if she were mine I'd soon put her into real flames."

The rest of the day went on in much the same way, and

the children found it more and more difficult to amuse their guest. It was astonishing to find how very soon she tired of any game. "What shall we do now?" was her constant cry; and it grew so tiresome that Nancy and the boys at last went off to play together, and left her entirely to Pennie. And this arrangement grew to be a settled thing, for it really was almost impossible to play the usual games with Ethelwyn; there was no sort of check on her overbearing ways, because "she was a visitor," and must do as she liked. Now, she was a very poor hand at "making up," and did not understand "Shipwrecks" or "Desert Islands" in the least; but this would not have mattered if she had been willing to learn. Joined, however, to complete ignorance on those subjects, she had a large amount of conceit, and seemed to think she could do everything better than anyone else. For instance, if they were going to play "Shipwrecks"—"I'll be captain," she would exclaim at once. This had always been Ambrose's part, and he rather prided himself on his knowledge of nautical affairs, gathered from a wide acquaintance with Captain Marryat's stories. He gave it up politely to Ethelwyn, however, and the game began. But in two minutes she would say: "I'm tired of being captain; I'd rather be Indian savages." Indian savages was being performed with great spirit by Nancy, but the change was made, and the game went on, until Ethelwyn cast an envious eye upon Dickie, who, with a small pail and broom, was earnestly scrubbing at the carpet, under the impression that she was a cabin-boy washing the deck of a ship. "*I* should like to be cabin-boy," said Ethelwyn.

But here the limit of endurance was reached, for Dickie grasped her little properties tightly and refused to give up office.

"*Me* will be cabin-boy," was all she said when Pennie tried to persuade her.

"You see she's so little," said the latter apologetically to Ethelwyn, "there's no other part she *can* take, and she likes the pail and broom so."

"Oh, very well," said the latter carelessly, "then I don't care to play any more. It's a very stupid game, and only fit for boys."

Things did not go on pleasantly at Easney just now, and the longer Ethelwyn stayed the more frequent became the quarrels; she had certainly brought strife and confusion with her, and by degrees there came to be a sort of division amongst the children. Pennie and Ethelwyn walked apart, and looked on with dignified superiority, while the others played the old games with rather more noise than usual. Pennie tried to think she liked this, but sometimes she would look wistfully after her merry brothers and sisters and feel half inclined to join them; the next minute, however, when Ethelwyn tossed her head and said, "How vulgar!" she was quite ashamed of her wish.

She wondered now how it was that she had been able to play with the boys so long without disagreement before Ethelwyn came. Of course these quarrels were all their fault, for in Pennie's eyes Ethelwyn could do no wrong; if sometimes it was impossible to help seeing that she was greedy and selfish, and even told fibs, Pennie excused it in her own mind—indeed, these faults did not seem to her half so bad in Ethelwyn as in other people, and by degrees she thought much more lightly of them than she had ever done before.

For Ethelwyn had gained a most complete influence over her, partly by her beauty, and partly by her coaxing, flattering ways. It was all so new to Pennie; and, though she was really a sensible little girl, she loved praise and caresses overmuch; like many wiser people, she could not judge anyone harshly who seemed to admire her.

So she was Ethelwyn's closest companion in those days, and even began to imitate what she considered her elegant manners. She spoke mincingly, and took short little stiff steps in walking, and bent her head gracefully when she said, "Yes, please," or "No, thank you." The new plush bonnet was a misery to her, and she sighed to be beautifully dressed.

Chapter Seven.
The Chinese Mandarin.

This uncomfortable state of things had been going on for nearly a fortnight, and Ethelwyn's visit was drawing to a close, when one morning there came a letter from Miss Unity. It contained an invitation to Pennie to stay three days at Nearminster, and ended with these words:

"If my god-daughter has her little friend still with her, I shall be glad to see her also, if she would like to come."

Now it happened that this suggestion of Miss Unity's came at a wonderfully convenient moment; for it had been arranged already that Ethelwyn's governess should meet her at the Nearminster station in three days' time, and take her back to London. She would now go from Miss Unity's house instead of from Easney, and Mrs Hawthorn was not at all sorry to think that the children would be separated a little earlier than was first intended.

So, with many cautions not to be troublesome, not to talk in bed, and not to touch the china, she told the little girls that they were to go to Nearminster. The news quickly spread through the family, and caused a deep but secret joy to the other children, for they were very tired of Ethelwyn; nevertheless they restrained any expression of their pleasure until the day of departure, when they gathered at the white gate to see the wagonette pass. The little girls were feeling even more dignified and grown-up than usual, for it was a great event to drive over to Nearminster quite alone; therefore it was all the more trying to be greeted by a derisive song:

"Hurray, hurray, hurray!
Ethelwyn is gone away!"

screamed the shrill voices, even Dickie doing her best to swell the chorus. It was so loud that it sounded a long way up the road; and Ethelwyn's favourite remark, "How very vulgar!" did not disguise it in the least.

The first day at Nearminster was fine and bright, and the children found plenty to entertain them. It was all new to Ethelwyn; and to Pennie, although she knew them so well, every object had an ever fresh interest. They went into the market with Miss Unity in the morning, and watched her buy a chicken, fresh eggs, and a cauliflower, which she carried home herself in a brown basket. Then in the afternoon Bridget was allowed to take the children into the town that they might see the shops, and that Pennie might spend her money. For she had brought with her the contents of her money-box, which amounted to fivepence-halfpenny, and intended to lay out this large sum in presents for everyone at home. It was an anxious as well as a difficult matter to do this to the best advantage, and she spent much time in gazing into shop-windows, her brow puckered with care and her purse clutched tightly in her hand. Ethelwyn's advice, which might have been useful under these circumstances, was quite the reverse; for the suggestions she made were absurdly above Pennie's means, and only confusing to the mind.

"I should buy that," she would say, pointing to something which was worth at least a shilling.

Pennie soon left off listening to her, and bent her undivided attention to the matter—how to buy seven presents with five pence halfpenny? It might have puzzled a wiser head than Pennie's; but at last, by dint of much calculation on the fingers, she arrived with a mind at rest at the following results:— An india-rubber ball for the baby, a lead pencil for father, a packet of pins for mother, a ball of twine for Ambrose, a paint-brush for Nancy, a pen-holder for David, and a tiny china dog for Dickie.

Ethelwyn was very impatient long before the shopping was done.

"Oh, spend the rest in sweets," she said over and over again in the midst of Pennie's difficulties.

But Pennie only shook her head, and would not even look at chocolate creams or sugar-candy until she had done her business satisfactorily.

In the evening she amused herself by packing and unpacking the presents, and printing the name of each person on the parcels, while Miss Unity read aloud. It was not a very amusing book, and Ethelwyn, who had spent all her money on sweets and eaten more of them than was good for her, felt cross and rather sick and discontented. She yawned and fidgeted, and frowned as openly as she dared, for she was afraid of Miss Unity; and when at last bed-time came, and the little girls were alone, she expressed her displeasure freely.

"I can't bear stopping here," she said. "It's a dull, ugly old place, I think I wish I was back in London."

"Well, so you will be the day after to-morrow," replied Pennie shortly. She did not like even Ethelwyn to abuse Nearminster, and she was beginning to be just a little tired of hearing so much about London.

Unfortunately for Ethelwyn's temper the next day was decidedly wet—so wet that even Miss Unity could not get out into the market, and settled herself with a basket of wools for a morning's work. Through the streaming window-panes the grass in the Close looked very green and the Cathedral very grey; the starlings were industriously pecking at the slugs, and the jackdaws chattered and darted about the tower as usual, but there was not one other living thing to be seen. "Dull, horribly dull!" Ethelwyn thought as she knelt up in the window-seat and pressed her nose against the glass. It was just as bad inside the room; there was Miss Unity's stiff upright figure, there was her needle going in and out of her canvas, there was the red rose gradually unfolding with every stitch. There was Pennie, bent nearly double over a fairy book, with her elbows on her knees and a frown of interest on her brow. There was nothing to see, nothing to do, no one to talk to. Ethelwyn gaped wearily.

Then her idle glance fell on the clock. Would it *always* be twelve o'clock that morning? And from that it passed to the Chinese mandarin, which stood close to it. He was a little fellow, with a shining bald head and a small patch of hair on each side of it; his face, which was broad, had no features to speak of, and yet bore an expression of feeble good-nature. Ethelwyn knew that the merest touch would set his head nodding in a helpless manner, and she suddenly felt a great longing to do it. But that was strictly forbidden; no one must touch the mandarin except Miss Unity; and, though she was generally quite willing to make him perform, Ethelwyn did not feel inclined to ask her. She wanted to do it herself. "If she would only go out of the room," thought the child, "I'd make him wag his head in a minute, whatever Pennie said."

Curiously enough Bridget appeared at the door just then with a message.

"If you please, ma'am," she said, "could Cook speak to you in the kitchen about the preserving?"

Now was Ethelwyn's opportunity, and she lost no time. She went quickly up to the mantel-piece directly Miss Unity closed the door, and touched the mandarin gently on the head.

"Look, Pennie! look!" she cried.

Pennie raised her face from her book with an absent expression, which soon changed to horror as she saw the mandarin wagging his head with foolish solemnity. Ethelwyn stood by delighted.

"I'll make him go faster," she said, and raised herself on tiptoe, for the mantel-piece was high.

"Don't! don't!" called out Pennie in an agony of alarm; but it was too late. Growing bolder, Ethelwyn gave the mandarin such a sharp tap at the back of his head that he lost his balance and toppled down on the hearth with a horrible crash.

There he lay, his poor foolish head rolling about on the carpet, and his body some distance off. Hopelessly broken, a ruined mandarin, he would never nod any more!

For a minute the little girls gazed speechlessly at the wreck; there was silence in the room, except for the steady tick-tack of the clock. Then Ethelwyn turned a terrified face towards her friend.

"Oh, Pennie!" she cried, "what *shall* I do?" for she was really afraid of Miss Unity.

Pennie rose, picked up the mandarin's head, and looked at it sorrowfully.

"Mother *told* us not to touch the china," she said.

"But can't we do anything?" exclaimed Ethelwyn wildly; "couldn't we stick it on? He's not broken anywhere else. See, Pennie!"

She put the mandarin on the mantel-piece and carefully balanced the broken head on his shoulders.

"He looks as well as ever," she said; "no one would guess he was broken."

"But he *is*," replied Pennie; "and even if he *can* be mended I don't suppose he'll ever nod like he used to."

"Are you going to *tell* her we broke him?" asked Ethelwyn after a short pause.

Pennie stared.

"*We* didn't break him," she said; "it was you, and *of course* you'll tell her."

"That I sha'n't," said Ethelwyn sulkily; "and if you do, you'll be a sneak."

"But you'll *have* to say," continued Pennie, "because directly he's touched his head will come off, and then Miss Unity will ask us."

"Well, I shall wait till she finds out," said Ethelwyn, "and if you tell her before I'll never never speak to you again, and I won't have you for my friend any longer."

"I'm not going to tell," said Pennie, drawing herself up proudly, "unless she asks me straight out. But I *know* you ought to."

As she spoke a step sounded in the passage, and with one bound Ethelwyn regained her old place in the window-seat and turned her head away.

Pennie remained standing by the fire, with a startled guilty look and a little perplexed frown on her brow.

Miss Unity's glance fell on her directly she entered; but her mind was occupied with the cares of preserving, and though she saw that the child looked troubled she said nothing at first.

"If Ethelwyn would *only* tell," thought Pennie, and there was such yearning anxiety in her face as she watched Miss Unity's movements that presently the old lady observed it, and looked curiously at her through her spectacles.

"Do you want anything, Penelope?" she asked, and as she spoke she stretched out her hand to the mantel-piece, for the mandarin was a trifle out of his usual place. She moved him gently a little nearer the clock; Pennie's expression changed to one of positive agony, and the mandarin's head fell immediately with a sharp "click" on to the marble! Clasping her hands, Pennie turned involuntarily towards Ethelwyn. Now she *must* speak. But Ethelwyn was quite silent, and did not even turn her head. It was Miss Unity's voice which broke the stillness.

"Child," she said, "you have acted deceitfully."

She fixed her eyes on Pennie, who flushed hotly, and certainly looked the very picture of guilt.

Of course Ethelwyn would speak now. But there was no sound from the window-seat.

Pennie twisted her fingers nervously together, her chest heaved, and something within her said over and over again: "I didn't do it—I didn't do it." She had quite a struggle to prevent the little voice from making itself heard, and her throat ached with the effort; but she kept it down and stood before Miss Unity in perfect silence.

The latter had taken the broken head in her hand, and was looking at it sorrowfully.

"I valued this image, Penelope," she went on, "and I grieve to have it destroyed. But I grieve far more to think you should have tried to deceive me. Perhaps I can mend the mandarin, but I can't ever forget that you have been dishonest—nothing can mend that. I shall think of it whenever I see the image, and it will make me sad."

The little voice struggled and fought in Pennie's breast to make itself heard: "I didn't do it, I didn't do it," it cried out wildly. With a resolute gulp she kept it down, but the effort was almost too great, and Miss Unity's grave face was too much to bear. She burst into tears and ran out of the room. Then hurrying upstairs she plunged her head into the side of the big bed where she and Ethelwyn slept together, and cried bitterly. Unjustly accused, disappointed, betrayed by her best friend—the world was a miserable place, Pennie thought, and happiness impossible ever again. There was no one to take her part—Ethelwyn was deceitful and unkind; and as she remembered how she had loved and worshipped her, the tears flowed faster. How could she, *could* she have done it? Then looking back, she saw how wilfully she had shut her eyes to Ethelwyn's faults, plain enough to everyone else. That was all over now: she had broken something beside the mandarin that day, and that was Pennie's belief in her. It was quite gone; she could never love her the least little bit again, beautiful and coaxing as she might be; like the mandarin, she had fallen all the lower because she had once stood so high.

Then Pennie's thoughts turned longingly towards home. Home, where they were all fond of her, and knew she was not a deceitful little girl. She was very sorry now to remember how she had neglected her brothers and sisters lately for her fine new friend, and how proud and superior she had felt.

"Oh," she cried to herself in a fervour of repentance, "I never, never will care so much about 'outsides' again! Insides matter much the most."

The next day passed sorrowfully for Pennie, who felt a heavy cloud of undeserved disgrace resting upon her. Whenever she saw Miss Unity glance at the empty space on the mantel-piece, she felt as guilty as though she really had broken the mandarin, and longed for an opportunity of justifying herself. But there was no chance of that; the day went on and Miss Unity asked no questions, and behaved just as usual to the little girls— only she looked rather sad and stern.

As for Ethelwyn, when she was once quite sure that Pennie would not "tell," her spirits rose, and she was lavish of her thanks and caresses. She pressed gifts upon her, and kisses, and was anxious to sit quite close to her and hold her hand; but Pennie was proof against all this now. It had no effect upon her at all, and she even looked forward with a feeling of positive relief to the next day, when she would say good-bye to the once-adored Ethelwyn.

And the time came at last; smiling, nodding, and tossing her yellow hair, Ethelwyn got into the train which was to take her away from Nearminster, and Pennie stood at Miss Unity's side on the platform, gazing seriously after her from the depths of the plush bonnet. In her hand she held almost unconsciously a large packet of sweets which Ethelwyn had thrust into it just before entering the carriage; but there was no smile on her face, and when the train had rolled out of sight, she offered the packet to Miss Unity:

"Please, take these," she said; "I don't want them."

That same afternoon Mrs Hawthorn and Nancy were to drive in from Easney and fetch Pennie home, and she stationed herself at the window a good hour before they could possibly arrive, ready to catch the first glimpse of Ruby's white nose. When, at length, after many disappointments, caused by other horses with white noses, the wagonette really appeared, she could hardly contain herself for joy, and was obliged to hop about excitedly. She was so glad to see them. There was mother, and there was Nancy, dear old Nancy, in the black plush bonnet, which was now a far more pleasant object to Pennie than the smart blue one she had lately envied. Now the carriage was stopping, and Nancy was lowering one stout determined leg to the step, clutching mother's umbrella and a doll in her arms. Pennie stayed no longer, but rushed down-stairs into the hall and opened the door. It might have been a separation of years, instead of three days, from the warmth of her welcome, and Nancy said presently with her usual blunt directness:

"What makes you so glad to see us?"

Pennie could not explain why it was, but she felt as if she had never really been at home during Ethelwyn's visit to Easney, and was now going back again—the real old Pennie once more. So she only hugged her sister for reply, and both the little girls went and sat in the window-seat together, while their mother and Miss Unity were talking.

But soon Nancy's observant glance, roving round the room, fell on the empty space beside the clock.

"Why!" she said in a loud voice of surprise, "where's the mandarin?" For she was very fond of the funny little image, and always expected to see him wag his head when she went to Nearminster.

Everyone heard the question, and for a minute no one answered. Then Miss Unity said gravely:

"There has been an accident, Nancy. The mandarin is broken. I fear you will never see him nod his head again."

"Oh, what a pity!" exclaimed Nancy. "Who did it?" Then turning to her sister with an alarmed face, "Was it you?"

"I *hope* not," said Mrs Hawthorn, leaning forward and looking earnestly at Pennie.

In fact everyone was looking at her just then—Miss Unity with sorrow, Mrs Hawthorn with anxiety, and Nancy with fear. How delightful it was to be able at last to stand straight up, and answer triumphantly with a clear conscience, "No!"

At that little word everyone looked relieved except Miss Unity, and her face was graver than before as she said:

"Then, Pennie, why didn't you say so?"

"You never asked me," said Pennie proudly.

Miss Unity's frown relaxed a little; she bethought herself that she really never had asked the child; she had taken it for granted, judging only by guilty looks.

"If it was not you, Pennie," she said gently, "who was it?"

"I can't tell that," said Pennie, "only *I* didn't."

"Then," exclaimed Nancy eagerly, "I expect it was that mean Ethelwyn."

Miss Unity took off her spectacles and rubbed them nervously; then she went up to Pennie and kissed her.

"I am sorry I called you deceitful, Pennie," she said, "but I am very glad to find I was wrong. When I look at the mandarin now, I shall not so much mind his being broken, because he will remind me that you are a good and honourable child."

Now the cloud was gone which had made Pennie's sky so dark, and all was bright again; the drive back to Easney, which she always enjoyed, was on this occasion simply delightful. Though the afternoon was dull and foggy, and there was a little drizzling rain, everything looked pleasant and gay from under the big umbrella which she and Nancy shared together; the old woman at the halfway cottage smiled and nodded as they passed, as though she knew that Pennie felt specially happy, and when they got to the white gate, there were Ambrose and David waving their caps and shouting welcome. How delightful to be at home again—without Ethelwyn!

Pennie rushed about, hugging everybody and everything she happened to meet, animals and human beings alike, till she became quite tiresome in her excess of joy.

"There, there, Miss Pennie, that'll do. Leave the child alone now, you'll make her quite fractious," said Nurse, rescuing Cicely from a too-energetic embrace. Pennie looked round for something fresh to caress, and her eye fell on the Lady Dulcibella sitting in her arm-chair by the dolls' house. There was a satisfied simper on her pink face, as though she waited for admiration; she held her little nose high in the air, and one could almost hear her say, "How very vulgar!" Pennie turned from her with a shudder, and picked up Jemima, who was lying on the floor flat on her face.

"Why, Pennie," exclaimed Nancy, opening her eyes very wide, "you're *kissing Jemima!*"

"Well," replied Pennie, giving the battered cheek another hearty kiss, "I feel fond of her. She's the oldest of all, and very useful I think she ought to be kissed sometimes."

Chapter Eight.
How Dickie went to the Circus.

"Has you ever seen a circus, Andoo?"

"Aye, missie."

"When has you seen it?"

"Years ago, little missie—years ago. When I was a fool."

"Is you fool now, Andoo?"

"Maybe, missie, maybe," (with a grim smile); "but I surely was then."

Dickie dismissed the subject for the moment, and turned her attention to the little green barrow full of sticks which she had just wheeled into the potting shed. There was a pleasant mingled scent of apples, earth, and withered leaves there; from the low rafters hung strings of onions, pieces of bass, and bunches of herbs, and in one corner there was a broken-backed chair, and Andrew's dinner upon it tied up in a blue checked handkerchief. Bending over his pots and mould by the window in his tall black hat, and looking as brown and dried-up as everything round him, was Andrew himself, and Dickie stood opposite, warmly muffled up, but with a pink tinge on her small round nose from the frosty air. She was always on good terms with Andrew, and could make him talk sometimes when he was silent for everyone else; so, although she very seldom understood his answers, they held frequent conversations, which seemed quite satisfactory on both sides.

Her questions to-day about the circus had been called forth by the fact that she had seen, when out walking with Nurse, a strange round white house in a field near the village. On asking what it was, she had been told that it was a tent. What for? A circus. And what was a circus? A place where horses went round and round. What for? Little girls should not ask so many questions. Dickie felt this to be unsatisfactory, and she accordingly made further inquiries on the first opportunity.

She laid her dry sticks neatly in the corner, and grasping the handles of her barrow, stood facing Andrew silently, who did not raise his grave long face from his work; he did not look encouraging, but she was quite used to that.

"Did 'oo like it, Andoo?" she inquired presently with her head on one side.

"Well, you see, missie," replied Andrew, "I lost the best thing I had there, through being a fool."

"Tell Dickie all about it," said Dickie in a coaxing voice.

She turned her little barrow upside down as she spoke, sat down upon it, and placed one mittened hand on each knee.

"Dickie kite yeddy. Begin," she said in a cheerful and determined manner.

Andrew took off his hat, and feebly scratched his head; he looked appealingly at the little figure on the barrow as though he would gladly have been excused the task, but though placid, the round face was calmly expectant.

"I dunno as I can call it to mind," he said apologetically; "you see, missie, it wur a powerful time ago. A matter of twenty years, it wur. It was when I lost my little gal."

"Where is 'oor 'ittle gal?" asked Dickie.

"Blessed if I know," said Andrew, shaking his head mournfully; "but wherever she be, she ain't not to call a *little* gal now, missie. She wur jest five years old when I lost her, an' it's twenty years ago. That'll make her a young woman of twenty-five, yer see, missie, by this time."

"Why did 'oo lose 'oor 'ittle gal?" pursued Dickie, avoiding the question of age.

"Because I wur a fool," replied Andrew frowning.

"Tell Dickie," repeated the child, to whom the "little gal" had now become more interesting than the circus; "tell Dickie all about 'oor 'ittle gal."

"Well, missie," began Andrew with a sigh, "it wur like this. After her mother died my little gal an' I lived alone. I wasn't a gardener then, I was in the cobblin' line, an' sat all day mendin' an' patchin' the folks' boots an' shoes. Mollie wur a lovin' little thing, an' oncommon sensible in her ways. She'd sit at my feet an' make-believe to be sewin' the bits of leather together, an' chatter away as merry as a wren. Then when I took home a job, she'd come too an' trot by my side holdin' me tight by one finger—a good little thing she was, an' all the folks in the village was fond of her, but she always liked bein' with me best—bless her 'art, that she did."

Andrew stopped suddenly, and drew out of his pocket a red cotton handkerchief.

"Why did 'oo lose her?" repeated Dickie impatiently.

"It wur like this, missie," resumed Andrew. "One day there come a circus to the village, like as it might be that out in the field yonder, an' there was lots of 'orses, and dogs that danced, an' fine ladies flyin' through hoops, an suchlike. Mollie, she wanted to go an' see 'em. Nothing would do but I must take her. I can see her now, standin' among the scraps of leather, an' the tools, an' the old boots, an' saying so pleadin', 'Do'ee take Molly, daddie, to see the gee-gees.' So, though I had a job to finish afore that night, I said I'd take her, an' I left my work, an' put on her red boots—"

"Yed boots?" said Dickie inquiringly, looking down at her own stumpy black goloshes.

"Someone had giv' me a scrap of red leather, an' I'd made her a pair of boots out of it," said Andrew; "they didn't cost me nothin' but the work—so I put 'em on, an tied on her little bonnet an' her handkercher, an' we went off. Mollie was frighted at first to see the 'orses go round so fast, an' the people on their backs cuttin' all manner of capers, just as if they wur on dry ground. She hid her face in my weskit, an' wouldn't look up; but I coaxed her a bit, an' when she did she wur rarely pleased. She clapped her hands, an' her cheeks wur red with pleasure, an' her blue eyes bright. She wur a pretty little lass, Mollie wur."

Andrew stopped a minute with his eyes fixed thoughtfully on Dickie, and yet as though he scarcely saw her. She hugged herself with her little crossed arms, and murmured confidentially, "Dickie will go to the circus too."

"There wur a chum of mine sittin' next," continued Andrew, "an' by and by, when the place was gettin' very hot, an' the sawdust the horses threw up with their heels was fit to choke yer, he says to me, 'Old chap,' he says, 'come out an' take a glass of summat jest to wet yer whistle.'

"'I can't,' says I, 'I've got my little gal to look after. I can't leave her.' But I *was* dry, an' the thought of a glass of beer was very temptin', 'no call to be anxious over that,' says he; 'you won't be gone not five minutes, an 'ere's this lady will keep an eye on her fur that little while, I'm sure.' 'Certingly,' says the woman sitting next, who was a stranger to me but quite respectable-lookin'. 'You come to me, my dearie!' and she lifted Mollie on to her knee an' spoke kind to her, an' the child seemed satisfied; an' so I went."

Andrew coughed hoarsely but went on again after a minute, speaking more to himself than Dickie—who, indeed, did not understand nearly all he had been saying.

"When I got into the 'Blue Bonnet' there wur three or four more of my chums a-settin' round the fire an' havin' a argyment. ''Ere,' says one, 'we'll hear what Andrew Martin's got to say to it. He's a tough hand at speakin'—he'll tell us the rights on it.' An' before I knew a'most I wur sittin' in my usual place next the fire, with a glass of beer in my hand. I wur pleased, like a fool, to think I could speak better nor any of 'em; an' I went on an' on, an' it wasn't till I heard the clock strike that I thought as how I'd left my little gal alone in the circus for a whole hour. I got up pretty quick then, for I thought she'd be frighted, but not that she could come to any harm. So I went back straight to where I left her with the woman, an'—"

"What does 'oo stop for?" said Dickie impatiently.

"She wur *gone*, missie!" said Andrew solemnly, spreading out his hands with a despairing gesture—"gone, an' the woman too! I've never seen my little gal since that day."

"Where is 'oor 'ittle gal?" asked Dickie.

"Lost, missie! lost!" said Andrew shaking his head mournfully. "I sha'n't never see her no more now. Parson he was very kind, an' offered a reward, an' set the perlice to work to find her. 'Twarn't all no good. So I giv' up the cobblin' an' went about the country doin' odd jobs, because I thought I might hear summat on her; but I never did, an' after years had gone by I come ere an' settled down again. So that's how I lost my little gal, an' it's nigh twenty years ago."

At this moment Nurse's voice was heard outside calling for Dickie, and Andrew's whole manner changed at the sound. He thrust the red handkerchief into his pocket, clapped his hat firmly over his eyes, and bent towards his work with his usual cross frown.

Dickie looked up with a twinkling smile as Nurse came bustling in.

"Andoo tell Dickie pitty story," she said.

"Ho, indeed!" said Nurse with a sharp glance at Andrew's silent figure. "Mr Martin keeps all his conversation for you, Miss Dickie, I think; he don't favour other people much with it."

On their way to the house Dickie did her best to tell Nurse all she had heard from Andrew; but it was not very clear, and left her hearer in rather a confused state of mind. There was something about a 'ittle gal, and red boots, and a circus, and something that was lost; but whether it was the red boots that were lost, or the little girl, was uncertain. However, Nurse held up her hands at proper intervals and exclaimed, "Only fancy!" "Gracious me!" and so on, as if she understood perfectly; and when Dickie came to the last sentence this was really the case, for she said in a decided voice:

"Dickie will go to the circus too."

"No, no," replied Nurse; "Dickie is too little to go—she will stay at home with poor Nursie and baby."

It seemed to Dickie that they always said she was too little when she wanted to do anything nice, but if ever she cried or was naughty they said she was too big: "Oh, fie, Miss Dickie! a great girl like you!" If she was a great girl she ought to go to the circus; and she repeated firmly, "Me *will* go," adding a remark about "Andoo's 'ittle gal," which Nurse did not hear.

At dinner-time there was nothing spoken of but the circus; the children came in from their walk quite full of it, and of all the wonderful things they had seen in the village. Outside the blacksmith's forge there was a great bill pasted, which showed in bright colours the brilliant performance of "Floretta the Flying Fairy" on horseback; there was also a full-length portrait of Mick Murphy the celebrated clown.

Even more exciting were the strange caravans and carts arriving in the field where the large tent had already been put up;

and Ambrose had caught sight of a white poodle trimmed like a lion, which he felt quite sure was one of the dancing-dogs.

The circus was to stop two days—might the children go to-morrow afternoon?

There was a breathless silence amongst them whilst this question was being decided, and mother said something to Miss Grey in French; but after a little consultation it was finally settled that they were to go. Dickie had listened to it all, leaving her rice-pudding untasted; now she stretched out her short arm, and, pointing with her spoon at her mother, said:

"Dickie too."

But Mrs Hawthorn only smiled and shook her head.

"No, not Dickie," she said; "she is too young to go. Dickie will stay at home with mother."

Now the vicar was not there—if he had been he would probably have said, "Let her go;" and Dickie knew this—it had happened sometimes before. So now, although she turned down the corners of her mouth and pushed up one fat shoulder, she murmured rather defiantly:

"Dickie will ask father."

The next day was Saturday—sermon day, and the vicar was writing busily in his study when he heard some uncertain sounds outside, as though some little animal were patting the handle of the door—the cat most likely—and he paid no attention to it, until he felt a light touch on his arm. Looking down he saw that it was Dickie, who, having made her way in, stood at his elbow with eager eyes and a bright flush of excitement on her cheeks.

"Please, father," she said at once, "take Dickie to see the gee-gees."

The vicar pushed back his chair a little and lifted her on to his knee. He would have liked to go on with his sermon, but he always found it impossible to send Dickie away if she once succeeded in getting into his study.

"What does Dickie want?" he asked rather absently.

"Please, father, take Dickie to see gee-gees," she repeated in exactly the same tone as at first.

The vicar took up his pen again and made a correction in the last sentence he had written, still keeping one arm round Dickie. But this divided attention did not please her; she stuck out two little straight brown legs and said reflectively:

"Dickie got no yed boots."

"No, no," said the vicar with his eyes on his sermon; "Dickie's got pretty black boots."

"Andoo's 'ittle gal got yed boots," pursued Dickie.

"Andrew's little girl! Andrew hasn't got a little girl," said her father.

For answer Dickie pursed-up her lips, looked up in his face, and began to nod very often and very quickly.

"Where is she, then?" asked the vicar.

Dickie stopped nodding, and, imitating Andrew as well as she could, shook her head mournfully, spread out her hands, and said:

"Lost! lost!"

"You funny little thing!" said the vicar, laying down his pen and looking at her. "I wonder what you've got into your head. Wouldn't Dickie like to run upstairs now?"

But she only swung herself backwards and forwards on his knee and repeated very fast, as if she were saying a lesson:

"Please, father, take Dickie to see gee-gees."

There was evidently no chance of getting rid of her unless this question were answered, and the sermon must really be finished. The vicar looked gravely at her and spoke slowly and impressively:

"If Dickie is a good little girl, and will go upstairs to the nursery directly, and *stay there*, father will ask if she may go and see the gee-gees."

Dickie got down and trotted away obediently, for she thought she had gained her point; but alas later on, when mother was appealed to, she was still quite firm on the subject—Dickie must *not* go to the circus. The four other children were enough for Miss Grey to take care of, and Nurse could not be spared—Dickie must stay at home and be a good little girl.

Stay at home she must, as they were all against her; but to be a good little girl was quite another thing, and I am sorry to say it was very far from her intention. If she were not taken to the circus she would be as naughty a little girl as she possibly could. So when she had seen the others go off, all merry and excited, leaving her in the dull nursery, she threw herself flat on her face, drummed with her feet on the floor, and screamed. At every fresh effort which Nurse made to soothe her the screams became louder and the feet beat more fiercely, and at last the baby began to cry too for sympathy.

Dickie was certainly in one of her "tantrums," and Nurse knew by experience that solitude was the only cure, so after a while she took Cicely into the next room and shut the door. For some time Dickie went on crying, but presently when she found that Nurse did not come back the sobs quieted down a little, and the small feet were still; then she lifted her face up from the floor with big tears on her cheeks and listened. Hark! what was that funny noise? Boom boom! boom! and then a sort of trampling. It was the circus in the field close by, and presently other strange sounds reached her ear. She looked at the door leading into the bed-room—it was fast shut, and Nurse was walking up and down, singing to the baby in a low soothing tone. Dickie got up from the floor and stood upright with sudden resolve shining in her eyes: she would go to the circus in spite of them all!

Fortune favours the disobedient sometimes as well as the brave, and she met no one to ask where she was going on her journey through the passages; when she came to the top of the stairs she saw that the hall was empty and silent too—only the dog Snuff lay coiled up on the mat like a rough brown ball. He had not been allowed to go to the circus either. She went slowly down, holding by the balusters and bringing both feet carefully on to each step; as she passed him Snuff opened one bright eye, and, watching her, saw that she went straight to the cupboard under the stairs, where the children's garden coats and hats were kept. There they hung, five little suits, each on its own peg, and with its own pair of goloshes on the ground beneath. Dickie's things were on the lowest peg, so that she might reach them easily and dress herself without troubling anyone. She struggled into the small grey coat, tied the bonnet firmly under her fat chin, and sat down on the lowest stair to put on the goloshes. Snuff got up, sniffed at her, and gave a short bark of pleasure, for he felt quite sure now that she was going into the garden; but Snuff was wrong this time, as he soon found when he trotted after her. Dickie had wider views, and though she went out of the garden door, which stood open, she turned into a path leading to the front of the house and marched straight down the drive. Through the white gate they went together, the little grey figure and the little brown one, and along the village street. It was more deserted than usual, for everyone was either in the circus or gaping at the outside of it, and Dickie and her companion passed on unquestioned. Soon they reached the field where the tent and some gaily-painted caravans stood; but here came an unexpected difficulty. Which was the circus? Dickie stood still and studied the question with large round eyes, and her finger in her mouth, Snuff looking up at her wistfully.

Nearest to them there was a large travelling caravan, with windows and curtains, and smoke coming out of a funnel in the roof; its sides were brightly decorated with pictures of horses, and of wonderfully beautiful ladies jumping through hoops, and there was also a picture of a funny gentleman with red patches on his face. This must be the circus, Dickie decided at last, and she proceeded to climb up the steps in front, closely followed by Snuff. The door was a tiny bit open, and she gave it a push and looked in. Things never turn out to be much like what we have expected, and it was so in Dickie's case, for what she saw was this:

A small room with a low bed in one corner, and a black stove, and pots and dishes hanging on the walls; a cradle with a baby in it, and by the cradle a pleasant-faced young woman sitting in a wicker chair sewing busily—so busily that it was quite a minute before she raised her eyes and saw the little grey-coated figure standing at the door with the dog at its side.

"Well, little dear," she said, "an' what do you want?"

Dickie murmured something, of which only the word circus was distinct.

"Is mammy at the circus?" asked the woman smiling; but Dickie shook her head decidedly.

"Why, bless your little 'art," said the woman, getting up from her chair, "I expect you've lost your folks. You come in and stay a-longer me till the circus is done, and then we'll find 'em. Jem 'ull be 'ome then. I'd go myself, but I can't leave the little un here."

Dickie began to pout in a distressed manner when the woman took her up in her arms; this was not the circus after all. But just as she was making up her mind to cry her attention was caught by something lying on the baby's cradle, and she held out her hand for it and said "Pitty!" It was a tiny roughly-made scarlet leather boot, rather faded and worn, but still bright enough to please Dickie's fancy. She chuckled to herself as the woman gave it her, and muttered something about "Andoo's 'ittle gal;" and presently, tired with her great adventure and made drowsy by the warmth of the little room, she dropped off to sleep on the woman's knee, with the boot hugged tightly to her bosom.

"Pretty dear! What a way her folks will be in!" said the woman to herself, and she laid Dickie softly on the bed and covered her with a shawl.

They were indeed "in a way" at the vicarage. When the circus party came back they found everyone in a state of most dreadful anxiety, and the whole house in confusion. Dickie was missing! Every crevice and corner was searched, and every place, likely and unlikely, that a child could be in. No Dickie. Could she possibly have gone into the village alone? It was getting dusk; there were strange people and tramps about—it was an alarming thought. Andrew must go at once and inquire at every cottage.

Andrew went, lantern in hand, and chin buried in his old grey comforter. "Had anyone seen Miss Dickie and the dorg that arternoon?"

No; no one had seen little missie. Always the same answer until he got to the circus field, where knots of people still lingered talking of the performance. Amongst these he pushed his way, making the same inquiry, sometimes, if they were strangers, pausing to give a description of Dickie and Snuff; and at last the answer came from a thin man with a very pale face, who was standing near the entrance to the tent:

"Right you are, gaffer. The little gal's all serene. My missus has got her in the caravan yonder."

Guided by many outstretched and dirty fingers, Andrew made his way up the steps and told his errand to the woman within. There was Dickie, sleeping as peacefully as though she were tucked up in her own little cot; Snuff, who was curled up at her feet, jumped up and greeted Andrew with barks of delight, but even this did not rouse her.

"There," said the woman, lifting the child gently, "you'd better take her just as she is, shawl an' all; it's bitter cold outside, an' you'll wake her else."

She laid Dickie in the long arms stretched out to receive her, and as she did so the shawl fell back a little.

"She's got summat in her hand," said Andrew, glancing at the little red boot.

"So she has, bless her," said the woman; "you'll mind an' bring that back with the shawl, please, mister. I set store by yonder little boot."

Andrew stared hard at the woman. "The vicar'll be werry grateful to you for takin' care of the little gal," he said. "What might be yer name, in case he should ax' me?"

"My name's Murphy," she answered, "Molly Murphy; my husband's Mr Murphy, the clown, him you see in the playbills."

Still Andrew stood with his eyes fixed on her face; then he looked from her to the little boot clutched so tightly in Dickie's fat fist.

"Might you 'appen to have the feller one to this?" he

asked.

"Surely," answered the woman. "Once they was mine, an' now I'm keeping 'em against my little gal's old enough to wear 'em."

She held out the other red boot.

"Is there—is there," asked Andrew hesitating, "two big 'M's' wrote just inside the linin'?"

"Right you are," answered the woman; "an' it stands fur —"

"It stands fur 'Molly Martin,'" said Andrew, sitting suddenly down on the edge of the bed with Dickie in his arms. "Oh, be joyful in the Lord, all ye lands! I set every stitch in them little boots myself', an' you're the little gal I lost twenty years ago!"

It really did turn out to be Andrew's little girl, grown into a young woman and married to Mr Murphy the clown. The whole village was stirred and excited by the story, and Andrew himself, roused for the moment from his usual surly silence, told it over and over again to eager audiences as he had to Dickie, only now it had a better ending.

The children at the vicarage found it wonderfully interesting—more so than one of Pennie's very best, and the nice part about it was that it had been Dickie who discovered Andrew's little girl. Indeed, instead of being scolded for disobedience as she deserved, Dickie was made into a sort of heroine; when she was brought home sound asleep in Andrew's arms, everyone was only anxious to hug and kiss her, because they were so glad to get her back again, and the next day it was much the same thing. The children were breathless with admiration when the history of the red boot was told, and Dickie's daring adventure, and Mrs Hawthorn was scarcely able to get in a word of reproof.

"But you know," she said, "that though we're all glad Andrew's daughter is found, still it was naughty and wilful of Dickie to go out by herself. She knew she was doing wrong, and disobeying mother."

"But if she hadn't," remarked David, "most likely Andrew never would have found his little girl."

"Perhaps not," said Mrs Hawthorn; "but it might not have ended so well. Dickie might have been hurt or lost. Good things sometimes come out of wrong things, but that does not make the wrong things right."

Still the children could not help feeling glad that Dickie had been disobedient—just that once.

And then another wonderful thing to think of was that Andrew was now really related to the clown, whose appearance and manners they had all admired so much the day before. That delightful, witty person, whose ready answers and pointed pleasantries made everyone else seem dull and stupid! He was now Andrew's son-in-law. It appeared, however, that Andrew was not so grateful for this advantage as he might have been.

"Aren't you glad, Andrew," asked Nancy, "that Molly married the clown?"

"Why, no, missie," he answered, scraping his boot on the side of his spade, "I can't say as I be."

"Why not? He must be *such* a nice man, and *so* amusing."

"Well," said Andrew, "it's a matter of opinion, that is; it's not a purfesson as *I* should choose, making a fool of myself for other fools to laugh at. Not but what he do seem a sober, decent sort of chap, and fond of Molly; so it might a been worse, I'll not deny that."

A sober, decent sort of chap! What a way to refer to a

brilliantly gifted person like the clown!

"An' they've promised me one thing," continued he as he shouldered his spade, "an' that is that they'll not bring up the little un to the same trade. She's to come an' live a-longer me when she's five years old, an' have some schoolin' an' be brought up decent. I don't want my gran-darter to go racin' round on 'orses an' suchlike."

"Then you'll have a little girl to live with you, just as you used to," said Pennie.

"And her name will be Mollie too," said Ambrose.

"But you won't take her to the circus again, I should think?" added David.

"Andoo's 'ittle gal had yed boots," said Dickie, and here the conversation finished.

The End.

Lightning Source UK Ltd.
Milton Keynes UK
UKHW020222081019
351185UK00008B/552/P